'You are the most surprising, the most wonderful thing that ever happened to me. But I must warn you. I am not a free man.'

'What do you mean?' Lucy asked.

'There is a saying in my village that when a man marries two women ————— time I will go back ————— you would not be ————— happens, when I go ————— between us must end.'

He had said it. As simply and as brutally as that.

She leaned forward, gently put her hand over his mouth. 'Marc, you have one big fault!'

He looked confused. 'I have?'

'Yes. You're talking too much. You're worrying too much. We'll wait and see how our lives go—live in the present, not the future.'

He frowned. 'Is it that simple?'

'It's that simple. And you could start living in the present by kissing me again.'

DELL OWEN MATERNITY

Midwives, doctors, babies—
at the heart of a Liverpool hospital

Dear Reader

Of all the departments in a large modern hospital, perhaps the most exciting, most difficult, most rewarding, must be the maternity section. What responsibility could be greater than knowing that only your skill and training can bring a new life into the world? What thrill could be greater than seeing proud parents carry away the child that you have helped be born?

The three heroines of these books are all dedicated to their work. They are trained in all aspects of maternity care—ante-natal, post-natal, delivery suite, SCBU and clinic. They find their careers deeply satisfying. But they are also young healthy women, who need further fulfilment outside work.

Sometimes it is difficult to separate your private and your work life. A hospital can be like a glasshouse, where emotions and feelings grow faster, grow more intense. My three midwives all think they have found love in the hospital—but there are problems. Work and love become intertwined, and it is difficult to sort out priorities, to decide exactly what feelings mean.

Love will always find a way. Our heroines find that that way can be a hard one—but in the end they triumph.

I hope you have enjoyed reading these stories; I enjoyed writing them.

Best wishes

Gill Sanderson

THE NOBLE DOCTOR

BY
GILL SANDERSON

MILLS & BOON®

First published in Great Britain 2005
Harlequin Mills & Boon Limited,
Eton House, 18-24 Paradise Road, Richmond, Surrey TW9 1SR

© Gill Sanderson 2005

ISBN 0 263 84348 3

Set in Times Roman 10½ on 12¼ pt.
03-1205-48720

Printed and bound in Spain
by Litografia Rosés, S.A., Barcelona

CHAPTER ONE

IT DIDN'T seem a year since Jenny's wedding, Midwife Lucy Stephens thought.

She looked at the carefully framed photograph on her wall. In the middle her friend Jenny, gorgeous in her long white dress—and sitting in her wheelchair. Two bridesmaids, herself on one side and on the other her friend Maria. And now Maria had found her man, had married wonderful Tom. Jenny had been a bridesmaid again.

Always a bridesmaid, never the bride! Who cared?

She remembered the conversation she had had with the Reverend Madeleine Hall. Lucy had just caught the bouquet that the bride had thrown. In fact, she'd caught half a bouquet. The great arrangement of maroon and lemon roses had been designed so that it would split in half. And the bridesmaids had caught a half each. 'You caught it, now you're supposed to get married,' Madeleine had said.

'Maria can go before me,' Lucy had said. And Maria had married first.

Lucy grinned. She wasn't worried, there was plenty of time. Life was good at the moment. She loved the city she lived in, she was enjoying her work as a midwife, she was learning more every day. She had a big family to support her, many friends and a full social life. Yes, life was good.

A one-year wedding anniversary present had to be

paper. Lucy carefully wrapped the pack of expensive writing paper she had bought, taped a card to the side of the pack. Now she could get ready.

It wasn't exactly a party. But Mike Donovan, Jenny's husband, had invited a few old friends and a few people from the department to a drink at the Red Lion. Just to celebrate one good year.

What to wear? Lucy opened her wardrobe, pursed her lips. It was only a casual drink but, still, a girl liked to look her best. The white sundress with the small silver pattern or light-coloured trousers and a darker vest top? Both would show off her summer tan. Then a few minutes on her hair and just a touch of make-up and— Her phone rang. Just when she had decisions to make. Slightly put out, Lucy reached for the receiver

'Hi, sweetheart,' a confident male voice said. 'Change of plan. I'll pick you up at your place and we'll walk over to the party together. I may be a bit late, so you'll have to wait for me.'

Simon Day. The junior registrar she'd seen something of during the past few weeks.

'I can walk there myself. We'll meet there as we arranged.' Her voice was cool. Confidence was a good thing for a doctor but you could have too much of it.

Simon didn't notice her lack of enthusiasm. 'I've got news for you,' he said. 'Well, really news for both of us. I've landed that job in America, working in Chicago. A great career move.'

She was pleased for him, he'd talked of nothing else for weeks. 'Simon, I'm so glad. When do you start?'

'In a couple of months. And there's something else. They say they're short of midwives at the moment.

You can come with me, we'll go as a couple. We could make an announcement tonight.'

'An announcement?'

'You know.' His voice was impatient. 'About us.'

Lucy blinked. What was this? A proposal? On the phone? Typical Simon. And it came to her with sudden and absolute clarity. Not only did she not want to go to America with Simon, she also didn't really want to see much more of him. He took too much on himself.

Still, she didn't want to be unkind. Gently, she said, 'Simon, I don't want to go to America. I love it here, with the work and my friends and my family. I'm a home girl. And about us going as a couple—we're friends but we aren't a couple.'

His voice grew irritated, as it always did when he didn't get his own way. 'Of course we're a couple. Everyone knows that.'

'If they know that we're a couple, it's because you've told them so. Whatever there might be between us, Simon, it's only just beginning.'

They had been for drinks together, gone to a concert, but that was all. He had walked her home a few times, kissed her outside the nurses' home. It had all been quite pleasant but...

'Is this an argument or is it an ending? Lucy, I won't be messed about.' Now Simon was seriously annoyed.

Lucy tried to be patient. 'It isn't an argument and it certainly isn't an ending, because nothing has really begun. Simon, I don't want to go to America with you but I'm sure you'll find someone who will.'

'If that's the way you feel.' Simon rang off.

Lucy sighed as she replaced the receiver. She won-

dered if she ought to feel guilty, then decided not. So
Simon was not for her. But, then, who was? Over the
past year she'd been out with perhaps half a dozen
men on casual dates. None had really attracted her.
Simon had been the best of them—but now that was
over she realised that she wasn't too bothered. Perhaps
she was too choosy, her standards too high? She decided not. Jenny and Maria had both done well. Somewhere there would be a man for her, and when she
met him it would be obvious. Or she'd remain happily
single.

Now, what had she been thinking before Simon had
phoned? What to wear? It was an informal party.
She'd wear the comfortable trousers and vest top.

It was a warm summer evening. Jenny's little party
had spilled out of the Red Lion and was sitting on
benches in the garden. Lucy kissed her friend and her
husband, gave them their present and accepted a glass
of white wine. Then she sat on the nearest bench and
talked to whoever was passing. She was among
friends, she loved this.

'Lucy, good to see you!'

Lucy squinted upwards. All she could see was two
figures outlined by the setting sun. One was obviously
John Bennet, the O and G consultant, she recognised
the voice. The other was just an outline.

'Hi, John, welcome to the party.'

John moved to one side so she could see him more
clearly. 'Before I join the festivities, I've got to have
a quick business talk with our celebrating couple,' he
said. 'So you can do me a favour. This is Marc
Duvallier, he's to be one of our new SHOs. Could you
look after him for a moment? Marc, this is Lucy

Stephens, just one of the superb midwives that really run the department. See you in a while.' And John was gone.

Lucy felt her hand taken, shaken gently. 'I am most pleased to meet you, Midwife Lucy Stephens,' a voice said. 'May I sit next to you?'

Their eyes locked, for a second, a minute, an hour—who knew? Then silently Lucy indicated that there was a place next to her on the bench. She wondered what was happening to her. She couldn't have spoken if she had tried. Marc Duvallier sat by her. The cheerful hum of conversations round about suddenly seemed distant, there was only herself and this man in a tiny bubble world of their own. She was bewildered, but she knew that her life would never be quite the same again.

All after meeting one man for just one minute?

He obviously wasn't English but he spoke the language perfectly, his voice low, almost husky. But there was a touch of something different about it. Lucy suspected that he was French. It was an attractive voice, it had a caressing feel to it, as if the speaker wanted you to be his friend—or even lover. She felt she wanted to sit by this man and just listen. Or just listen and look, because he was the most astounding man she had ever... She caught herself, tried to drag herself back into the real world. He was just a very attractive man with a deep voice. She would probably have to work with him. They'd get to know each other and—

'I'm afraid I am a gatecrasher to the party,' Marc said. 'I am not due to start work for another week, but I came to introduce myself. And Mr Bennet told me that this was a small celebration, that I should meet many of the people I would be working with. Please, what are we celebrating?'

A direct question. Now she'd have to talk. Somehow Lucy collected her whirling thoughts, forced herself to speak.

It was a long story to tell. Lucy thought she'd have to cut it short. 'It was so romantic, I cried because I was so happy. That man over there, Mike Donovan, it's a year since he married my friend Jenny. She's the woman who is holding his hand. She got married in a wheelchair the morning before having an operation on her spine, which would decide whether she'd ever walk again. She said that she didn't want to think about getting married until they both knew the result of the operation. Mike wanted to get married before the operation—to show he didn't care what the result was. So we arranged a surprise ceremony. Mike just turned up, told her she was getting married and she had to go along with it. That was exactly a year ago. And now she couldn't be happier. Isn't that wonderful?'

'A truly romantic story. And, I see, a romantic story with a happy ending. That is not always the case. Now, I see you have finished your drink. May I fetch you another and then perhaps we can talk about romance a little more?'

He smiled at her, showing that this was a joke—but Lucy still felt dizzy.

'No, you're the guest here...Marc. I'll go to get us both something.'

He shook his head. 'We have met for the first time. I will buy your wine, that is proper. I will be only a moment.'

He took her assent for granted, she noticed, but she

didn't feel as angry as she had when Simon had tried to make decisions for her earlier. Somehow, with Marc, it was different.

She watched him stride through the cheerful crowds of her friends, rather glad of the respite. She needed a minute to pull herself together, to work out what was happening to her. This was ridiculous!

She was twenty-five, a mature, trained, experienced midwife. Without being arrogant, she knew that she was attractive—well, enough men had told her so. She liked the company of men, had had men friends before, she felt at home in their company. One or two men she had seriously thought she might in time come to love.

But never had she felt the sudden rush of electric attraction that she had felt for Marc Duvallier. She felt a moment of panic. How was she going to cope with this entirely new emotion? It wasn't just that he was the most attractive man she had ever met. When for that first moment they had gazed into each other's eyes she had felt an instant kinship. It sounded foolish, but it was as if they had been made for each other, that they had been waiting for this moment all their lives. Or was that just what she felt? How could she be sure that he felt the same way? Lucy moaned quietly to herself. She didn't know. He could even be married!

This was madness!

He was walking back towards her now, followed by a waiter carrying a tray with a silver bucket and two glasses. He did not go unnoticed, Lucy saw several admiring glances and guessed that when he came back to talk to her it would not be long before they were interrupted. Well, that was both a good thing and a bad thing. She needed to get her breath, to make sense of what was happening. And she couldn't do it in his presence.

Perhaps thirty seconds before he greeted her again. She took a great breath, expelled it slowly. She would be calm. Friendly but calm. Even if it killed her.

She watched him approach and tried to be detached. Look at him, weigh him up, as if he were just another colleague.

He was dressed formally in a dark suit and white shirt, with some kind of club or medical tie. Entirely proper dress to meet his new colleagues. He hadn't known he'd be coming to a party. Lucy didn't know too much about men's clothes, but these clothes looked expensive.

But that wasn't it. Clothes didn't make the man. She knew a couple of consultants who dressed equally expensively—and they made no impression on her at all. This man dressed well, as if it was his right. She thought to herself that he would look good even if he was dressed in scrubs.

His hair was dark, and fairly long. In an essentially masculine way, he was good-looking. He had a lean face, high cheekbones, a mouth, she suspected, that could turn instantly from its present amiable sensuality to thin-lipped anger. His eyes were the darkest grey, and when she looked into them she felt that he could know at once what she was thinking.

These days it was not in her nature to be overwhelmed by a man. It was not in her nature to be overwhelmed by anyone or anything. But she had to admit—Marc Duvallier was overwhelming. She wasn't sure if she liked that.

He arrived at their table, smiled at her and she decided that, yes, she did like him being overwhelming.

She watched as the waiter took a bottle of white wine from the silver bucket, expertly uncorked it then poured a little into one of the glasses. Marc sipped the wine and nodded to the waiter. 'That is fine, thank you.' The waiter half filled the two glasses, then left.

Marc turned to Lucy and said, 'I hope you don't mind, but I bought a bottle of wine,' he said. 'It's a Sancerre, I'm very fond of it. The wine from behind the bar was…all right, but I thought that perhaps since this is a special day it ought to be marked by a special wine.'

'Why is this a special day?' Lucy croaked. What if he said, 'Because I've met you'?

But he didn't say that—well, not exactly. Instead he said, 'I am meeting the people who I will work with for the next year or so. Colleagues, and perhaps in time friends. For me it will be a time of discovery and perhaps adventure. May I offer you a glass of wine?'

She took the glass and tasted the wine. It was easy to tell that this was different from the cheerful plonk that she usually drank. 'To your future here,' she said, touching her glass to his.

'To our future here,' he corrected. For a moment they were both silent. Lucy wondered if he was thinking the same as she was. That it would be more than nice if they had a future.

It struck her that she was as silent as a tongue-tied schoolgirl and that wasn't like her at all. She had to say something. 'You're not English, are you?' she asked. 'Though you speak it perfectly.'

'I come from the south-east of France,' he said. 'But I spent much of my schooldays in England. My mother sent me here. And then eventually I decided to study medicine here.'

That voice! What it could do to her! It was like being stroked by the softest of fur.

'So you'll finish up working in England?'

He frowned. 'No, I am needed at home, in France. I'm looking forward to going back.'

Lucy wondered when he said that. He didn't seem to say it with much conviction.

'Aren't you a bit old for an SHO?' She knew that this was rather personal but she needed to know about him.

He didn't seem to mind the question. 'I am indeed. But in the middle of my course I had to drop out to work with my family for three years. I like to think that the experience of real life has made me a better doctor.'

'You see enough real life in hospital. Soon you'll—'

'A bottle of wine? I see you're doing a good job of looking after Marc,' a cheerful voice said, 'but I'm afraid I've got to steal him now. He has other people to meet.'

Startled, Lucy looked up. There was John Bennet, and with him were Mike and Jenny. What did they want?

'I'm afraid that I've been monopolising Lucy here,' Marc said as he stood. 'But I look forward to meeting the rest of my new colleagues. Lucy, we will meet again quite soon.'

'I hope so,' she said. 'Marc, your wine…'

'Please, drink what you wish yourself, share the rest with your friends,' he said. 'Perhaps I'll see you before you go. I do hope so.'

Then, urged by John, he was gone, Mike by his side. Jenny came to sit next to Lucy.

'Since it's been offered, I'll taste that wine,' Jenny

said, producing her own glass. 'What do you think of our new SHO? Easy to tell that he's French, isn't it?'

'Very easy,' Lucy said. And then, as casually as she could make it, she asked, 'What do you know about him? Is he married or anything?'

Jenny shrugged. 'I don't know but I don't think so. He's getting one of those hospital doctor's flats, and they're only supposed to be for one person. You could always ask him.'

'I couldn't! He might think that I…that I wanted to know because I was interested and…' She stopped, unable to continue.

'But you are interested,' Jenny pointed out. 'With looks like that, a girl would have to be mad not to be interested. Besides, I know you, Lucy. I can tell what you're feeling.'

'Perhaps I am a bit interested,' Lucy mumbled. 'But I've only just met the man. He just seems pleasant and I like his voice and… Nice wine, isn't it?'

'It's wonderful wine,' Jenny agreed, 'and, yes, if you want we can change the subject.'

Lucy tried to rally her confused thoughts. 'I'm not sure what I'm thinking,' she said. 'But tell me what's it feels like to be an old married woman. I can't believe it's a year.'

Jenny stretched out her arms and smiled. 'Being married is better than I could have dreamed,' she said. 'It's wonderful. Find the right man and you'll be happier than you thought possible.'

'So it's just a question of finding the right man? Hmm. I'll remember that. Is finding the right man easy?'

'You'll know it when it happens.'

Jenny looked up across the lawn at the happily mingling crowd of her friends and then said, 'Finding the right man. Is this one a possibility? I've seen you together.'

Lucy looked up and sighed. Walking towards them, glass in hand and with a determined expression on his face, was Simon Day.

'Simon is not the right man,' she said. 'I'll just have to convince him of it. You won't see us together again.'

And then Simon was in front of them. 'Jenny, congratulations on a year's marriage,' he said. 'It's good to see you so happy.'

'Thank you, Simon. I'm happy because I'm with my friends.'

Simon obviously felt he had now done all that was necessary to be courteous. He said, 'This is a bit important, Jenny. I wonder if you'd mind leaving Lucy and me alone for a minute.'

Expressionless, Jenny looked at Lucy. Lucy nodded slightly. 'I'll go, then,' Jenny said, 'Lucy, we still have more talking to do.'

'This won't take long,' Lucy said, and watched as her friend walked away.

Simon sat by her, slid along the bench and tried to take her hand. 'Perhaps it's my fault and if so, I'm sorry,' he said. 'But I think we've got things a bit wrong.'

She pulled her hand away, thinking that he didn't look very sorry. 'I would say we've got things just right.'

Simon didn't know it, but he had picked the wrong time to speak to Lucy. She had been enjoying talking to Jenny, happy in her vague thoughts of what might happen in the future. With Simon came an unpleasant reality.

'You must understand, this is a great opportunity for me—for us, in fact. You'd like working in Chicago and—'

'I might like working in Chicago but I'm not going. Not with you. Simon, I told you, things are over between us.'

'You just don't mean that.'

Simon reached for the bottle of wine and started to pour himself a generous drink. When his glass was half-full Lucy reached over and took the bottle from him, set it down with a thump. 'That's not your wine,' she said. 'Neither is it mine.'

So now, inevitably, Simon got angry again. 'Off with the old love and on with the new,' he said. 'I saw you chatting up the new French guy, you and most of the nursing staff here. Look at them fawning on him. Like flies round...'

Lucy did glance across the lawn and Simon was right—there were rather a lot of females clustered around John and Marc. She tried to pretend to herself that it didn't irritate her a little. But perhaps her reply was unnecessarily sharp. 'Simon, you're boring me. Looking back, I think you've always bored me. Now, go away. There's nothing more I want to say to you, just goodbye. Is that clear enough?'

He looked at her disbelievingly. 'I think you'll be sorry you said that,' he said. 'Goodbye, Lucy.'

He walked away from her, his back rigid with anger. Lucy sighed. He had been right. She was sorry she had been unnecessarily cruel. But then...perhaps he had deserved it.

*   *   *

It was a good party. Lucy knew practically everyone there but some people she hadn't seen for a month or two and it was good to catch up on the gossip. And much of the gossip—among her nurse friends—was about the new arrival. Marc Duvallier had certainly caused a stir. And it wasn't because of his medical abilities.

She spoke to him a couple more times. But on each occasion they were in one of the little groups that kept forming and re-forming, just as they did at all parties. She wondered, did he seem to want to speak to her in particular? It seemed that way, though he was courtesy itself to everyone who spoke to him. Were most of his questions addressed to her? She wished she had him on her own again, as she had when he had first arrived.

But then she reminded herself that he was here for a year or so. There'd be plenty of chances for them to talk together at work. If he wanted to, that was. And she desperately wanted him to want to.

Simon hadn't left the party. But every time he appeared to be moving towards Lucy, she walked away to another group of friends. She didn't want to talk to Simon again, it would spoil her evening. Besides, he seemed to be drinking far too much.

Finally, it was time to go. After Jenny and Mike left, the party seemed to not have much point. And she was on earlies next day. A few seasoned drinkers were staying behind, and John still seemed to be deep in conversation with Marc. Well, if she was leaving, she could interrupt to say goodbye. Taking a breath, she went over to where the two men were sitting on one of the benches. Both stood as she approached.

'Time to get my beauty sleep,' she said. 'Marc,

good to meet you and I hope you'll be happy here
with us.'

'If I am made as welcome on the wards as I have
been here tonight, I shall indeed be happy. Lucy, it
was also so good to meet you.'

His grip was gentle, his hand warm, and as his
thumb stroked the back of her offered hand she wondered if the tiny caress was accidental or meant to
convey a hidden message. Whatever, it made her
shiver with delight.

'Good to see you here, too, John,' she said, and felt
entitled to hug the older man.

'Have to keep an eye on my charges,' John said
with a grin. 'Nobody's to enjoy themselves unless I'm
there as well. Goodnight, Lucy.'

She would have liked to stay longer but there was
no good reason to. One last glance at Marc and then
she turned and walked away. There would be other
days she could see him, she told herself. Then she
frowned. What was she thinking of? She knew nothing
about the man—he could be married, engaged or even
not interested in her.

But there had been that spark of recognition, that
flash between the two when they had first met. She
was sure she hadn't mistaken that. She smiled contentedly to herself. Suddenly her future seemed
brighter than it had done in a while. There were possibilities. And then she heard Simon call her name
from behind her.

The walk from the Red Lion to the nurses' home
led through a shrubbery. In the twilight Simon suddenly appeared alongside her, obviously he had been
running after her.

'We've got to get things right between us, Lucy,'

he said, reaching for her arm. 'We mean too much to each other to let a little thing come between us.' His speech was slurred.

'We mean nothing to each other.' She wriggled to evade his grasp. 'Simon, you're drunk, just go home and sleep it off.'

'I may be drunk but I know what I want. What you want. Now, I'm going to walk you home and we'll talk and you can make me some coffee and then—'

'I think that perhaps you misunderstand. Miss Stephens has already agreed that I would accompany her home.'

Lucy blinked, turned to see a dark figure that had walked silently up to them. Marc Duvallier? She didn't quite know what to feel—either pleasure at seeing him or anger that he should see her having this vulgar row with Simon. And why was her heart now beating so quickly? It certainly wasn't because of the argument with Simon, she could deal with him.

'I didn't know that! And I don't believe it either. You just—'

Lucy walked over and took Marc's arm. 'We missed each other at the party,' she told Simon, 'but we have things to discuss. Now, if you will excuse us.'

'But I need to—'

'Good evening, Dr Day,' Marc said. 'Perhaps you should leave now. I understand Midwife Stephens worked a full shift today before the party, she must be tired.'

Lucy couldn't make it out. Marc's voice had been calm, quiet. What he had said was true and had seemed to be quite unexceptionable. But both she and Simon had felt the undercurrent of menace in the words.

She glanced from one to the other, now little more

than outlines. Simon's shoulders were hunched, his arms held away from his sides, hands tightly clenched. A man under stress. By comparison, Marc seemed completely relaxed, at ease. Such a difference!

'Goodnight, Simon,' she said. Then she gently pressed Marc's arm and they walked on together. Simon didn't move and soon was lost in the twilight.

'Perhaps it was wrong of me to intrude,' Marc said, 'but I saw him leave after you walked away and guessed that he might be a little…awkward. I came to see if I might be able to help.'

'I could have dealt with him.' Lucy said honestly, 'but thank you for your help anyway. Much appreciated.'

'It was nothing. Now, I doubt there will be any more trouble from Dr Day. You'll be quite safe. But may I escort you to your home?'

At times there was something old-fashioned about his speech, and she was reminded that he was French. And she liked it. He showed her a courtesy that was sometimes missing in the men she mixed with. He treated her like a lady, not like a colleague.

'I'd be glad if you did walk me home,' she said. 'As you say, Dr Day won't reappear—but I'd like to chat to you.'

'That will be pleasant.' There was a moment's silence and then he asked, 'Dr Day—is he a particular friend of yours?'

She had to be honest. 'He wanted to be a particular friend and we have seen something of each other over the past few weeks. But earlier today I finished it. He made plans about our future without consulting me. I won't be taken for granted. And I don't like drunks.'

'Neither do I,' said Marc.

And then they paced on in apparently amiable silence for a while. But Lucy was worried, bewildered at the way things were going. She wasn't sure of what to say, apprehensive of saying the wrong thing. She liked Marc very much, but there was a definite foreignness about him. She couldn't tell what he was thinking, what he expected of her. It added to his attraction but it made being with him just a little harder.

'I like your pendant,' he said after a while. 'What does it say?'

She fingered the gold disc that hung from a chain round her neck. 'It was a twenty-first birthday present from my parents,' she said. 'It's Latin. It says, "*Amor vincit omnia*".'

'Love conquers all,' he translated. 'And is that something you believe?'

'Yes,' she said flatly. 'Don't you believe it?'

'I think I do,' he said. 'But there are many kinds of love.'

They reached the front door of the nurses' home and she felt almost in a panic. She didn't know what to do. If she invited him to her room, he might think it forward of her. If she didn't invite him, he might think it unfriendly. She was all right with English men, but French men were an unknown quantity. Perhaps she should—

Lucy, you're going mad, she thought.

Then he settled the problem. 'I will wait here till I see you safely inside,' he said. 'I have enjoyed our walk and our talk and I look forward to seeing more of you. I was a little frightened of coming here, it's good to know that I have at least one friend.'

He offered her his hand again. As he took hers, did he hold it a bit longer than was necessary? Perhaps that's what the French did.

'Yes, a friend,' she gabbled. 'See you soon I hope. Goodnight, Marc.' And she ran inside the building.

Once in her room she collapsed on the bed. Her first thought was simple. She had wanted him to kiss her. Her second thought was that she had to get a grip on herself. Too much had happened tonight, she would have to think about things, work out how she felt.

All this over one man? She hadn't felt this way since she'd had a schoolgirl crush on a pop star.

She didn't feel tired in the slightest, but knew she must be. She had been looking forward to the party, looking forward to enjoying herself. She had enjoyed herself, but had not expected to come home in this state of anxiety. She'd fallen for a man. But they'd only just met and she knew nothing about him. What was to come?

She felt restless, got undressed and showered, made herself a warm drink and still felt restless. Aimlessly, she picked up one of the pot plants on her window-ledge, a miniature red rose, and started to pull off the dead leaves. And from schoolgirl days came a memory of pulling the petals off a daisy, a form of divination. 'He loves me, he loves me not,' she muttered to herself, 'He loves me, he loves me not.'

It was unfortunate. She had pulled off all the dead leaves and it had left her with, 'He loves me not.' Lucy stared gloomily at the plant, and then pulled off a perfectly healthy leaf. She cursed and put her finger in her mouth. She'd pricked it. But, still, sometimes it was necessary to make sacrifices. Now he loved her.

Marc walked back across the hospital grounds, his head bent. Starting a new job was usually both exhausting and exhilarating. There were new people to meet, new protocols to master, a new workplace to get to know. He had been looking forward to it—in fact, he still was.

But now there was Lucy. He'd never met a Lucy before in his life, had never met a girl who had attracted him so instantly. It wasn't just that she was calmly beautiful—though the willowy figure, the perfect face and above all those wide grey eyes had drawn the attention of all who'd seen her. Perhaps it was because she seemed so full of life. And she was happy because her friends were happy—that was good.

And something had passed between them. Both had known it, both had felt it. The question was, what could he do about it?

He would like to see much more of Lucy, but he knew it could be difficult. He was not his own master. And he sensed that Lucy would expect—demand even—a total commitment. And that he couldn't offer. He was going to hurt her—or hurt himself.

Marc cursed silently to himself. For the moment only his native language would do to express his feelings.

CHAPTER TWO

BACK to work early next morning.

For a while Lucy had been working in the antenatal ward, she quite liked it. There were a few mums-to-be here who were just being kept in overnight, looking forward to a trouble-free birth. But mostly the patients were those having multiple births, those suffering from placenta praevia, those with pre-eclampsia, polyhydramnios, oligohydramnios. Most births took place without incident, but it was as well to be reminded that things weren't always simple.

And Jenny had taught her that the personal touch was just as important as the medical processes. Lucy felt that an important part of her job was to reassure the anxious, fearful mums-to-be. And she knew she was good at that. She was cheerful, chatty.

She walked into the nurses' room ready for handover. And there, dressed in scrubs, listening carefully to Melissa Spain, the sister in charge, was Marc Duvallier.

Lucy's first thought was that she had been right. Marc looked as attractive in scrubs as he did in a suit. Her second thought was to wonder what he was doing there. Almost automatically her hands went to her hair, now fastened in a tight, neat pleat. She smoothed the front of her uniform, wished she had put on just a touch more make-up.

But, still, what was Marc Duvallier doing here, now

dressed in scrubs, standing in the nurses' room, apparently waiting for handover? And why were all these midwives and nurses looking at him so casually—and so often?

The room was now full, time for handover. Melissa explained. 'I'd like to introduce Dr Duvallier, one of our new SHOs. Officially he will be starting in a couple of days, but John has invited him to look round for a day to get to know the work and us. I'll be talking to him for a while first and then he'll come round to see how we work.'

Marc stood up and when he spoke Lucy felt a flutter of interest among the female staff. 'I am looking forward to working with you all. I expect to learn from you. I have always thought that the doctor and the midwife were equally important, two sides of the same coin.'

That's good, Lucy thought in a detached way. He knew what to say. And he seemed sincere.

She knew that he had seen her come in but so far he hadn't acknowledged her presence. That again, she thought, was a good idea. They would have a chance to talk later. And when handover was finished and the midwives were trooping out and no one would notice, he looked up and smiled at her. It was a special smile, a smile that promised something. Lucy walked down the ward with more than the usual bounce in her stride.

Her first job was to do the observations on a patient suffering from diabetes. Diabetes and pregnancy did not go well together. There was the constant risk of hypertension. This woman needed a close eye kept on her. But, fortunately, so far things weren't too bad.

Just as she finished writing up her observations, the

door to the sister's office opened and Melissa came out. 'Can you deal with a new admittance coming up from A and E, Lucy?' she asked. 'Doesn't sound too serious. The woman is about thirty weeks and fell in front of a car. A and E have patched her up and we'll keep her in overnight for observation.'

'No problem,' said Lucy. 'There's a bed ready.' She smiled to herself. The speed with which A and E got rid of anything to do with childbirth was legendary. 'Are there any special problems?'

'Apparently she doesn't speak much English.'

Lucy sighed. This was not going to be easy.

She was waiting by the ward door when the patient came in. It was good to welcome people, make them feel instantly at home. The double doors opened.

A young woman in a wheelchair, she couldn't have been much older than nineteen. There was a great bruise down the side of her pale face and a row of sutures over the corner of her eye.

'Hello,' said Lucy, 'I'm Lucy Stephens. I'm a midwife and I'm going to make you comfortable and see that that baby of yours is all right. What's your name?'

'Name is…Astrid.'

The nurse handed Lucy a set of notes. 'Astrid is French.' She moved closer to Lucy and whispered, 'We can't find out anything about her. Either she doesn't understand or she doesn't want to tell us. She just keeps quiet.'

'We'll cope,' Lucy said brightly. 'Somehow we'll cope.' But it was hard.

She helped Astrid into bed, fastened the monitor to her. 'This is to see how your baby is doing,' she explained.

Astrid looked at her wide-eyed but said nothing.

There was no wedding ring on her finger. Lucy went on, 'Can we get in touch with your partner? Or is there any family?'

That was a word Astrid understood. 'Family...*famille*? No!' She shook her head and then winced, the movement making her head hurt. 'Is no *famille*.'

We'll see about that, Lucy thought, but said nothing. She did the usual observations, and mother and baby seemed to be fine. Then she checked Astrid's notes. Mild abrasions, cut to the head, no sign of concussion. Recommended twenty-four-hour stay for observation. If Astrid had not been pregnant, she would probably have been discharged.

Lucy tried again, speaking slowly. 'Is there nobody we can tell that you're here?'

Once again the blank, frightened look, the lack of reply. Lucy smiled and patted her hand. 'I think I know someone who can help us,' she said. 'Won't be a minute.'

She walked down the ward and knocked on the sister's door. It was shut today, which was unusual. Melissa opened the door and didn't seem pleased to see her.

'I need a French speaker,' said Lucy. 'I've got a patient who is French and speaks no English. And I think she's got problems.'

'I'll come at once,' a voice behind Melissa said. 'That is, if you want me to, Midwife Stephens.'

'I'll come, too,' Melissa said.

Marc appeared, standing behind her. For a moment he rested a hand on Melissa's shoulder. 'No need to,

Melissa,' he said. 'Three around a bed might frighten
the patient. May I suggest just Midwife Stephens here
and myself?'

'Whatever you say, Marc—Dr Duvallier.'

He has made an impression, Lucy thought. He's
even made an impression on the hardened Sister Spain.
Will he make an impression on everyone?

This was not the time for anything personal between
them. She walked back down the ward with Marc,
gave him a quick report on the patient. 'I've got no
problems with her physical state. We could probably
discharge her tomorrow morning after the registrar has
seen her. She gave an address which is in the middle
of student-land, probably a bedsit somewhere. But
there's no sign of a student card. She was unconscious
when brought in and the A and E staff looked through
her handbag, looking for some signs of identity. And
there was nothing. No letters, no credit cards, no pass-
port, nothing to show who she is. Just fifty pounds and
some change.'

Marc had an instant effect on Astrid. Perhaps it was
the cheerful smile he gave her, perhaps it was the flow
of gentle sounding words in her own language. Whatever, she smiled for the first time. But then she began
to look cautious. Perhaps Marc was too persuasive.
Lucy had taken GCSE-level French and then forgotten
everything. She could pick out a word here and there
but that was all.

After a while Marc stopped speaking and looked
expectantly at Astrid. Astrid said nothing. Marc re-
peated what he had said, and Lucy realised it had been
a question. And slowly, falteringly Astrid replied.
Marc reached out and touched her on the shoulder.

Then he turned and said quietly, 'Do you think you could fetch Astrid some juice, Lucy?'

'Not too strong,' Lucy said, and then went to fetch the drink. Marc had somehow worn down the girl's resistance. It wasn't just that he spoke her language. There was something both powerful and comforting about his manner.

And he changed when he spoke French. Partly it was that he used his body, his hands to communicate. And French was such an expressive language! It felt as if he was stroking her with words, calming and yet exciting her at the same time…Lucy shook her head in annoyance. This was silly!

When she came back with the coffee, Marc and Astrid were deep in conversation and looked up at her as if she were an intruder. 'I'll leave you for now,' Lucy said coolly. 'Dr Duvallier, if we could have a word when you've finished speaking?' She had other duties.

He came to see her ten minutes later.

'Astrid Duplessis,' he said. 'Aged nineteen, home is in small town in Brittany. About seven months ago, just after Christmas, she met an English student who was staying in a hostel in the village, trying to improve his French. They fell in love. Her parents found out— apparently they are very religious, perhaps rather narrow-minded. They didn't approve. And Astrid is an only child. So they sent her away to stay with relations on the other side of the country for a month, didn't even let her say goodbye to the boy. And when she returned her lover had gone.'

'And she's now nineteen! Parents must have more influence in France than they have here!'

He shrugged. 'France is a big country. Some country districts are remote from the cities. They have their own ways of doing things. This I know because…' He stopped, shook his head as if vexed and went on, 'She does not want to go back to her parents, she has her pride.'

'Pride won't feed a baby. What is she doing here now?'

'Somehow she persuaded her parents that she was coming here on a course. She didn't dare tell them that she was pregnant, she knew what they would say, how their reputation in the town would be ruined. She wanted to find her lover. But she has no address for him, isn't even sure of his full name. She knew him just as Kevin. And he has dark hair.'

'He's got dark hair, is called Kevin and might be a student here,' said Lucy. 'Well, that narrows the field down to two or three thousand. And I doubt he wants to be found anyway.'

Lucy wasn't being cynical. She was thinking of other, similar cases she had come across.

Marc didn't agree with her. 'Not necessarily so, Lucy! This Kevin didn't want to be parted from her, it was done before she could tell him. He must think that she deserted him. And she is sure that he loves her!'

'Now, where have I heard that before?' Lucy said. Then she stopped herself saying more.

But he had noticed her wry comment. He said, 'And I hope you will hear it again and that it will be meant.'

'Perhaps,' she said. 'It's just that…here in O and G we get too many cases of girls who think they have a future and then their partners just disappear.'

He nodded. 'I agree. Fathering a child, even by accident, brings responsibilities. And those responsibilities should be honoured!'

Lucy looked at him, a little surprised at his stern tone. 'You seem to feel as strongly about it as I do.'

'I am pleased we agree. There are duties in life as well as pleasures.'

This was a side of Marc Lucy hadn't yet met. And she thought she liked it. Too many of the young doctors of her acquaintance took refuge from the tragedies they came across at work in an easy cynicism. Marc had principles and wasn't afraid to show them.

'We can still hope for a happy ending,' she said, 'even if we know it's not too likely. Now, what do we do about Astrid?'

He was formal. 'You are the midwife in charge. If I may, I would like to visit her again tomorrow, perhaps just for a chat.'

'It'll make my job easier,' she agreed.

She didn't have a chance to say much more to him for the rest of her shift. From time to time she saw him across the ward, but they were busy at different tasks. Then, half an hour before handover at two o'clock, he came over to speak to her.

Now she had learned to recognise that thrill of anticipation when he came towards her. But she still liked it.

'Lucy, I gather you're to leave now. Are you on the same shift tomorrow?'

'Working earlies again,' she said. 'Will you be here again?'

'I regret, no. And this afternoon I have part of my

induction, I shall be busy until quite late. But tomorrow is Saturday and I too have the afternoon off. I wonder...would you like to show me something of your city? I know you are fond of it and I am a stranger here. And perhaps we could have dinner.'

Her heart thumped at the prospect. But then she remembered. 'Marc, I'd love to. But in the afternoon I'm meeting my sisters at the park, we're having a picnic and a children's birthday party. My nephew Dominic is six and he's mad on trains. And there's a little train in the park.'

He shrugged and smiled, and for a moment she thought he had never seemed more French. 'I do not wish to interfere with Dominic's birthday treat. No matter. Perhaps another time.'

'I'm free in the evening,' she pointed out, and was excited when she saw the obvious pleasure in his face.

'Excellent! May I pick you up at the nurses' home at about six?'

She thought for a moment and then shook her head. 'Not at the nurses' home. It would be all over the hospital within minutes.'

He was still smiling. 'You do not wish to be the subject of gossip?'

The way he looked at her, the sound of his voice and the way he seemed to concentrate all his attention on her made her feel as if she was the most special person in the world. But she had to be cautious. 'No. I'll pick you up at the doctors' flats, they're much quieter. And I'll drive you.'

Then something struck her. 'You don't object to being driven by a woman?'

He shook his head. 'Not at all.' Another smile. 'You are a good driver?'

'I'm wonderful,' said Lucy.

Then there was a plaintive cry from the nearest bed, and Lucy hurried away. She was still at work.

Marc had to leave before handover. Lucy walked across the grass to her home, her heart singing. Marc had asked her out. Perhaps they had a future, perhaps things would develop—who could tell?

Once in her room she looked at the rose plant she had dead-leaved. It was her imagination, of course it was her imagination. But the flowers seemed to be blooming more than ever.

A small disappointment next morning. There was a message from Marc, relayed to her by an apparently equally disappointed Melissa Spain. Dr Duvallier could not come to the ward to speak to Astrid Duplessis. But he gathered that Astrid was to be kept in, and he would call in another day. No matter. Lucy was seeing him that evening.

Lucy was to meet her two older sisters, Jan and Lizzie, in the park. Between them Jan and Lizzie had six children. It was Dominic's birthday, he had asked for a trip on the little train and a picnic. So that's what he was going to get.

There was just enough time to wrap Dominic's present, sign his card and hastily make a box full of small sandwiches. Then walk the mile or so to the park. Fortunately it was a fine day—though the three had prepared a contingency plan in case it rained.

She found the little party easily, there were a lot of people to kiss. Then she was enrolled to play ring a ring of roses. It was an exhausting game and as usual everyone screamed with laughter. Lucy was enjoying herself, she loved being with her family. There were children to play with, gossip to catch up on. And finally time to eat and have a rest.

Then something happened that she was not at all expecting.

She was sitting on a blanket, her back against a tree and a towel on her lap, giving a bottle to six-month-old Frances. Lizzie whispered, 'Look at that man. Isn't he gorgeous?' Then her voice rose a little. 'Good Lord, he's coming over here. Do you know him?'

Lucy looked up, she did know the man. It was Marc Duvallier.

As ever, he was dressed elegantly, this time in light chinos with a dark blue polo shirt. But this outfit showed more of him, the muscular arms and slim waist that before had been suggested were now quite obvious.

He stood above them, his expression doubtful. 'I have to apologise,' he said. 'I know I'm intruding. But I had nothing to do, the sun was out and you'd told me about this park. So I came for a walk round.'

'Great,' said Lucy. 'It's really good to see you.' And it was. She was shocked, she'd never felt this way quite so quickly. 'Look, I can't get up or talk much because Frances will soon be asleep. But these are my sisters, Lizzie and Jan, and these are all my nephews and nieces.'

'It's good to meet you all,' said Marc, shaking hands with Jan and Lizzie.

'Sit on a rug and have a sandwich,' said Lizzie.

Lucy thought that it was tactful—but typical—of

him that he spent most of his time talking to her sisters and their children. She was content to sit and hold Frances and look at him. She could tell, he was charming Lizzie and Jan. It wasn't a conscious act, he just showed that he was pleased at his welcome.

Lizzie was telling him about how they were a close family, how they all lived near each other, were constantly in and out of each other's homes. Lucy noticed that he didn't say anything about his own home. She thought it a bit odd.

After a while he said, 'I must confess, I'm going to work a lot with Lucy and I hope to learn from her. So I'm hoping to get on with her family.' From his pocket he took a small package. 'Lucy showed me the list of engines that Dominic has got. If you don't mind, I've bought him another. A small birthday gift.'

Nobody did mind, especially Dominic.

And so they talked for another ten minutes, then Jan said, 'I think it's train trip time now. Lucy, will you stay here and look after Frances? I don't want to disturb her unless it's necessary. Or did you want to come on the train yourself?'

'I've been on it before,' said Lucy.

So the excited children led the mothers away and Lucy was left alone with Frances and Marc.

He smiled. 'It was good to see you all together. You are a…happy family.'

She wondered why he had paused before saying 'happy'. 'Why did you come?' she asked.

There was silence for a moment. Then he said, 'I just wanted to see you. I've seen you at work, and at a party, but tonight I suspect I shall see you through the eyes of a…' He grinned. 'There is only one word for what I wish to say, it is a French word. I shall see you as a *boulevardier*.'

'You mean like that man who sang "Thank Heaven for Little Girls" in the film?'

'Not quite,' he said. 'But now I wanted to see you as a family person. And you are just as attractive here.'

'I see,' said Lucy, not quite sure that she did.

Frances had stopped feeding now. Lucy leaned the baby over her arm and was gently rubbing her back. 'You handle that baby with considerable expertise,' Marc said. 'May I try?'

He leaned over to take Frances. Cautiously, Lucy handed her over. 'Be careful,' she said. 'There's a towel here for your lap. She seems a bit disturbed and…'

But Marc had taken the baby and was already rubbing Frances's back. Frances burped once and then was sick all over Marc's polo shirt. 'I should have paid more attention to you,' Marc said calmly.

At first Lucy was horrified. She looked at the stained polo shirt, the oblivious baby, the towel in her lap. What had been an intimate little scene between them was now ruined. But then she saw his entirely calm face and she couldn't help it. She burst out giggling. 'Now you know what midwives, nurses and mothers have to go through,' she said.

'I had some idea already. No matter, these things happen. Have you got any wipes for Frances's face?'

'I'll see to her now, you're in enough of a mess.' She took Frances, settled her safely on the towel and reached for the baby bag. 'Now, take that shirt off and in a minute I'll take it and rinse it. There's a big toilet block over there.'

He crossed his arms, carefully pulled the shirt over his head. Lucy glanced at his bare chest, and then lowered her head. She had known it, his body was magnificent! Not an ounce of fat, and two wings of dark hair rose from the taut waist to the broad chest muscles. The thought of being close to that chest, held by those muscular arms… She had a baby to deal with!

He stood, the scrunched-up polo shirt in his hand. 'No need for you to do my laundry,' he said, 'and there are enough bare-chested men around for me not to be conspicuous. I'll go and wash this through.'

'Right,' muttered Lucy. 'Marc, I'm sorry she vomited all over you and I'm sorry I laughed at you.'

He bent, stroked the side of Frances's cheek. 'It doesn't matter. And I can have a shower before I meet you later. You don't want a companion smelling of baby vomit.'

'You could be accompanying a midwife who does just that,' she said.

Twenty minutes later the rest of the party returned. Marc stood as they approached—as Lucy had known he would. Lizzie and Jan eyed his naked chest. 'A half-naked man. What has been happening here?' Lizzie asked cheerfully.

'A small accident,' Marc said. 'Nothing to worry about. How was the train ride, Dominic?'

'Ace,' said Dominic, who tended to ration words.

'Good. Now, I've gatecrashed your party long enough, I should go. Lizzie, Jan, I do hope we'll meet again. Lucy, till tonight.'

'We'll boulevard together,' said Lucy. And then, greatly daring, she added, '*À bientôt*, Marc.'

He raised his eyebrows but said nothing.

'He's gorgeous,' Jan said as they all watched his retreating figure. 'Will he take you off to France, Luce? We want you here but we'll all come there for holidays.'

'Don't be silly. I only met him for the first time two days ago.'

'You can know he's the man for you after the first meeting,' Lizzie said, a reflective smile on her face. 'I know I did. And you're seeing him again tonight, aren't you?'

'And he's mad on you, too,' said Jan. 'It showed in his eyes. But…'

'But what?' Lizzie asked.

Jan frowned. 'When we were talking about our lives together he looked sad. Well, thoughtful if not sad. But he's still gorgeous.'

What should she wear? Bathed and hair dried, Lucy stood in her newest, most dainty underwear and looked thoughtfully at her wardrobe. It wasn't an easy choice.

She'd never had this problem before—she picked something and if it was the wrong choice, so what? But that had been before she had met Marc. Before Marc? It seemed such a long time ago, and yet she'd only known him two days. But in those two days he'd been seldom out of her thoughts.

What would a lady *boulevardier* wear? They were going to walk—stroll perhaps. So she felt she needed sensible shoes. Well, sensible-ish. But he had also said they would go to dinner, so something rather smart.

Eventually she settled on a cream linen trouser suit.

She looked well in it. But a coat as well, in case it got cold. She decided on her military-style mac. She looked in her full-length mirror and tried a smouldering expression. Hmm. It went quite well with her white balconette bra and brief lacy knickers. If he could see her now he…

She blushed at the very thought and quickly got dressed.

There were only four doctors' flats, in a little block some distance from the nurses' home. He must have been looking out for her as the front door opened before she reached it.

'Lucy! It's so good to see you. Just for once I'll lapse into my native language. *Chérie, tu es si belle!'*

'Sweetheart, you are so beautiful,' she translated. 'Marc, that's the nicest way I've ever been greeted.'

'Then I am pleased.' He stepped aside, waved her in. 'I am ready but I need my coat. For a moment, perhaps you might like to see the chaos I am at present living in. But in time all will be neat.'

She had been in the flats before. They were just adequate, furnished sparsely but with very little sense of style. She peered into the kitchen, the living room, the bedroom, noted the cases and cardboard boxes stacked in the hall.

'I am not going to unpack just yet,' Marc said. 'To live in such dismal surroundings would depress me. When I have two days' rest time I shall paint the walls a far more cheerful colour and buy myself a few things to turn this place into a home.'

She didn't know why she said it. 'I'll help you,' she said. Then she blinked. That had been a bit forward.

'I would so much like you to help,' he said slowly. 'You could make these dreary rooms come alive.'

Then he shook himself, as if to move onto other thoughts, and said, 'I need my jacket and then we can go. Where are you taking me, Lucy?'

'I'll take you wherever you want to go,' she said.

From the way his dark eyes flashed at her, she knew that he had received the half-subtle message. But he decided not to act on it, which perhaps was a good thing.

He took a jacket from the back of a chair, slipped it on, pulled it till he was comfortable. Lucy surveyed him, lips pursed. A pure white open-necked shirt, light fawn trousers, a dark blue linen jacket. He was magnificent! She felt glad she had gone to a little trouble to select her own clothes.

'*Chérie, tu es…tu es…*' She could see him smiling at her. 'I only got a C in GCSE-level French,' she said in exasperation, 'it makes things difficult. Got it! *Chérie, tu es beau!*'

He took her hand, lifted it and kissed it. 'A compliment I shall treasure.'

Did he know the effect of his lips on her hand? The shiver of delight that ran down her spine? She suspected he did.

He released her hand and said, 'Now, you told me you'd take me wherever I wished to go. At home I live in mountainous country, where there are many waterfalls. Could we perhaps walk by the river? A real river, with ships and the sea in the distance?'

'I know just the place,' she said.

The promenade wasn't far from the hospital. She drove him there, they parked the car and walked along the riverside path. There was a great expanse of silver water, a somehow romantic oil refinery on the distant opposite bank, the sight of Welsh hills in the distance.

'This is pleasant,' he said. 'Trees and parkland so close to the city centre.'

Lucy laughed. 'It used to be called the cast-iron shore,' she said. 'I don't know why. And then it was a rubbish dump. And then the council landscaped it and now it is wonderful.' She waved her hand at the river. 'This place is full of history. A hundred years ago ninety-five per cent of the world's shipping was registered up this river. And now...' She shrugged.

'All things change, and many are for the better. But for the moment we must be happy rather than philosophical. Tell me about your family, Lucy. I liked them so much. And you are so good with children.'

'I love my family and I love children.'

'Then why none of your own?'

She grinned. 'In time. I'm still only young. But I've got plans. I want four children altogether. And I have to find a man first.'

Both of them were joking, she told herself. This was just a playful conversation, not to be taken seriously.

'You have to find a man? What do you want in a man? And are you actually looking?'

'I'm not concentrating on finding a man, life's too full, too good for that. But I'll recognise him when he turns up. I know I will.'

'What kind of man? Tall or short? Dark or fair? Doctor, teacher, businessman, artist?'

'He could be anything,' she said breathlessly, 'but I'll know. I'll know the man I want to be father of our children.'

'And will he know it?'

'He will. Or there will be trouble.'

'So you are a romantic?'

'I suppose I am,' she said after a while. 'You know the way when you put a newborn baby on its mother's breast? You see that sudden access of mother love. It's so new, so intense, it's often frightening, that's why they often cry. Well, I want a love like that.'

'I have seen what you describe and it is wonderful. But it's only hormones.'

'No, it's not!' Then she thought for a moment and acknowledged, 'Well, I suppose hormones are part of it. But the hormones belong to people.'

She stopped walking, put her hands on the rail and watched a tanker, incredibly low in the water, pushing its way upstream.

'Why am I telling you all this? I don't usually gabble.'

'Perhaps because we're different,' he said. 'And opposites always attract. But you're not gabbling. What you say is true and it's beautiful.'

He reached over and took her hand, and they walked on slowly together. She felt comforted, happy to hold his hand. But there were things that she had to say.

'I want to know about you.'

'Ask whatever you wish, Lucy. I will answer if I can. If I cannot answer, I will say so.'

He frowned as he said that and she wondered what kind of things he would not be able to answer, but didn't ask. 'First, how old are you?'

'I am twenty-nine.'

'Why aren't you married, engaged, have a woman

waiting for you?' Then added anxiously, 'I take it there isn't such a woman?'

He shook his head decisively. 'There is no such woman.'

'Then why has no one grabbed you before now?'

'As you know, hospital life is frantic.' He shrugged. 'I must tell you, I have had affairs but they were mostly essentially casual. I hope that every time we parted, no one was hurt.'

'So do I,' said Lucy. 'Were you hurt at all?'

He thought a minute. 'Perhaps a little,' he said. 'I still get Christmas cards from a couple of them.'

'You said they were mostly essentially casual. You're sure that there's never been one special girl? The one who might be the one?'

He sighed. 'There was one who might have been special. Genevieve. A doctor slightly older than me. I thought for a while that things might have been…but then there was an *impasse*… Perhaps fortunately, she was offered a job in Australia that was too good to turn down. So we parted and I hear that now she is married.'

Genevieve. Lucy wanted to hear more of her. She thought that there was more to the story than Marc had told her. But she said, 'It all seems a bit over-casual to me. I couldn't do it. Don't you ever feel that life, feelings are overtaking you?'

His answer was ambiguous, Lucy didn't know what to make of it. 'Not so far,' he said.

'I wouldn't want a relationship that ends in sending Christmas cards.'

'There is something we must talk about, but perhaps not now. There is a problem.'

Now it was his turn to stop and stare, this time downriver towards the sea.

'I am not attached to a woman but I am to a place. My life is marked out. I come from the mountains of south-eastern France. Eventually I must return there.'

'Doesn't seem like much of a problem to me,' Lucy said.

'Perhaps not. But now the sun is shining, I am walking with a beautiful woman, we have the rest of the evening ahead of us and we are happy. Let us remain so. Dark, serious talk can wait.'

As he had done before, he took her hand to his mouth, kissed it. 'Now, will you take me to see the centre of the city?'

CHAPTER THREE

SHE was driving him to the city centre when his mobile phone rang. 'I am sorry, Lucy,' he murmured, but he answered it anyway.

'Dr Duvallier here. Yes John. Well, I am with someone, I was going out to dinner, but...' With his spare hand he felt for her shoulder, squeezed it. Then, reluctantly, he said, 'Yes, I suppose I am available... Take the train down tonight!' His voice rose. There was a long period when he was silent and then he said, 'It's very good of you to organise it for me, John. I'll go back to my room at once to pack.'

There was silence in the car, then Lucy said, 'I take it that our dinner has just been cancelled.'

'That was John Bennet. There's a three-day conference in London on new techniques in childbirth, which would be of tremendous use to me. It starts early tomorrow morning. Someone in the city has just dropped out, John thought of me and grabbed me the place. Lucy, I'm so sorry and I know I ought to—'

'Marc! It's only a dinner and three days, against a real opportunity for you. Of course you've got to go. I would be angry if you did anything else, I really would.'

'But are you also sorry to miss the rest of the evening?' His voice was quiet.

So was her reply. 'Very sorry.'

She pulled up at traffic lights, he took one of her hands and once again kissed it. For how much longer is he going to kiss just my hand? she thought. But she said nothing.

They drove back to the hospital, he had an hour to pack. And nothing she could say would persuade him to let her drive him to the station. 'I will order a taxi. I will be back soon, *chérie*. And then there are things we must talk about. Partings on station platforms are always painful, inconclusive affairs.'

It was a foolish, pointless thing that she said, but she said it. 'You will come back, though?'

And for the first time he kissed her. Quickly, lightly, on the lips. 'I will be back for you,' he said.

He phoned her the next two nights, but the calls were inconclusive and unsatisfactory. The first time he rang her mobile when she was having tea at her parents', and it was difficult to go outside in mid-meal. The second time she was on the ward, and as ever things were hectic. He just had time to say that he was missing her, and that the course was long and intensive, but was very worthwhile.

But he had phoned her, he was thinking about her. That was good enough for three days.

It was eight at night, things were quiet on the ward, the sister had slipped out somewhere for a few minutes. Only Lucy and Brenda, a middle-aged midwife, were present, and they were drinking tea in the nurses' room. And Marc walked in.

Lucy looked at him, unable to speak, her heart thudding in her chest. She had expected to see him the next day and she would have been prepared then. But here he was and all she could do was stare at him, open-mouthed.

He waved papers at them. 'I know I'm not expected,' he said, 'but I got back early from my course and it's straight into work. I gather that we've got three Caesarean sections due tomorrow, I've got to get consents.'

It was apparently a casual, professional remark. But he looked at Lucy and she knew he had come to see her.

'I'll take you to them,' Lucy said, making an attempt to be casual, 'I've finished my tea.' She ignored the knowing smile on Brenda's face. There was no need for it, gossip would be all over the hospital soon enough.

Their hands touched as they walked down the ward, but nothing was said. There was no need and, besides, they were at work. They smiled at the group sitting in their dressing-gowns and gazing at the wall-mounted TV. Lucy stood there listening as Marc explained the procedure and why a written consent was necessary.

If a mother elected to have a Caesarean section, she had to be advised of the possible dangers and then asked for her written consent. This simple job was usually left to the SHO.

She thought Marc did it well. Too many young doctors hurried through the necessary details, gave no time for questions. Marc really wanted the patient to understand what was involved.

It was always when things seemed to be quietest that trouble started.

The first mum-to-be happily signed. They moved on to the second patient and Marc had just started his explanation when the emergency buzzer sounded. And at the same time there was a scream—a scream of real pain. Marc and Lucy ran down the ward to where the emergency light was flashing.

'The baby's coming!' the woman screamed. 'The baby's coming, I can feel it now.'

No time for delicacy. Lucy threw back the bed covers. Oh, yes. The baby was coming.

'This is Margaret Elland, thirty-eight weeks,' she said quickly to Marc. 'She's your third Caesarean patient, this was to be her second section. First child was CPD—cephalo-pelvic disproportion. In labour for eighteen hours and baby got stuck. Not surprising, he was a good ten pounds. Braxton-Hicks' contractions this afternoon but nothing abnormal. Baby appears to be a good size on palpation but certainly not too big.'

Marc nodded, then stepped up to stand by the woman's head. 'Hi, I'm Dr Duvallier and this is Midwife Lucy Stephens. Now, baby seems to be in a bit of a hurry to be born, but we don't want you to worry. Lucy will help you and all will be well.'

Lucy noticed that even in this emergency, the words seemed to calm the patient. 'Fetch me a delivery pack,' she said.

Brenda appeared at the doorway, took in the situation at a glance. 'I'll fetch the resuscitaire and then bleep for the paediatrician.' She looked at Marc. 'Do you want the obstetric registrar?'

'No,' said Marc, 'but crash-bleep the paediatric team, there's mec-stained liquor.'

Lucy heard him mutter, 'And I hope they get here in time.'

The baby was born—the quickest Lucy had ever seen. And she—it was a little girl—was covered with sticky, black-green meconium. That meant trouble. Lucy quickly cut the cord but didn't, as she usually did, hand the baby to the mother. Instead, she passed her to Marc, who placed her in the resuscitaire that Brenda had just wheeled up.

The two jobs could now be divided. The baby was now the concern of Brenda and Marc, Lucy could concentrate on treating the mother. The placenta was still to be delivered and after such a speedy birth there was the ever-present risk of haemorrhage. But Lucy desperately wanted to know how the baby was progressing.

'Where's my baby? I want to see my baby!' the mother cried.

'Baby's passed meconium inside you and we need to make sure she hasn't got it into her lungs. Doctor's looking after her now.' She hoped everything was going to be OK. Meconium inhalation could be very serious.

There was time to risk a glance behind her. There were Marc and Brenda bent low over the resuscitaire, the combined cot and trolley that held almost everything to help the unnaturally quiet baby. Something in their posture told Lucy that all was not well. She heard Brenda whisper, 'This is severe birth asphyxia. Don't you think we'd better wait for the paediatrician?'

'We haven't got time. I've given her an Apgar score of four. I can see meconium below the vocal cords. I'm going to intubate her, otherwise we'll just push the meconium into her lungs.'

'Have you ever done it before?'

'If I don't do it now, the baby will die.'

Lucy knew what Marc had to do. First he would slide a laryngoscope down the baby's throat. Then he would be able to see as he slid the endotracheal tube through the trachea, and inside that a fine suction catheter to clear the trachea. Then the tube would be connected to an oxygen supply. And then the baby could breathe. And live. It wasn't usually a job for an SHO.

But Lucy still had her own work to do. There was the mother to be reassured, the placenta to be delivered. With the mother, things were all now normal. And then behind her she heard the clatter of rapid feet on the ward floor. The paediatric team had arrived. There was the murmur of voices and after a few minutes the registrar appeared by her side. He smiled down at the mother.

'Mrs Elland? I'm the paediatric registrar here. Your little girl has given us a couple of anxious moments but she seems to be OK now. We're going to take her down to our specialist care unit, probably just for the night. But before we do we'll wheel her in here and you can have a look.'

'Can I hold her?'

'After tonight you can spend a lifetime holding her. But she's resting now so we'll not disturb her. Don't worry. She's in good hands.'

The registrar left and Brenda appeared beside her.

'If you like, I'll take over here now. Emergency over and you look as if you need a rest.'

'Where's…?' Lucy asked weakly.

'The SHO went off with the paediatric team. They invited him to come along.'

'Right,' said Lucy.

Marc came back when there was only twenty minutes of the shift to go. An SHO's job was never finished, he had still to get one consent for a Caesarean section. And Brenda took him for a quick word with Mrs Elland.

Then it was handover time. But he was waiting when Lucy had changed and was ready to go home. 'I thought we might walk over together,' he said.

'That would be nice. And you can tell me all about our bit of excitement on the ward and then about the course.' They left the building and paced along one of the paths.

'We took baby Elland to SCBU,' he said. 'The registrar said that since I had started on the case, if I wanted to, I could continue. So I did.'

Lucy smiled. 'I heard what you were doing,' she said. 'You saved that baby's life, didn't you?'

He thought for a moment, then said, 'Probably. The registrar said I did.'

'And how do you feel now?'

He smiled. 'I've been in Britain a long time, I should have learned your habit of understatement, your fear of showing emotion. But I haven't. I'm French, I feel the Latin way and I can say what I feel. Lucy, I feel so good that I could…that I could…' Suddenly, he stopped, took her head between his hands. He pulled her to him and kissed her. A full-blooded kiss that sent her senses reeling. Then, slowly, he released her. 'I feel so good that I could kiss you,' he whispered.

'You just did. And that's British understatement.'

It was their first real kiss.

It had been so good—so unexpected but so good. For the moment she couldn't deal with it. So she took refuge in talking about work, talking about what had just happened.

'You took a risk in intubating the baby,' she said. 'SHOs shouldn't do it unless supervised, you would have been quite in order to wait until the Paeds team arrived. You knew they were on the way. Even if the little girl had died, you'd have done the proper thing. But if she had died after you intubated her, there'd have been all sorts of trouble.'

'I know,' he said. 'And I'll admit, I was scared. But if you feel that things have got to be done then you have to do them, no matter what the cost.'

'I see,' she said.

She felt that he was telling her about more than the baby being born, he was telling her about his view of life. And it frightened her slightly.

They passed under a newly lit lamp, she glanced up at his face. There were lines round his eyes, the unmistakable signs of fatigue. 'Aren't you tired?' she asked. 'The course in London and then the train journey and then this. You've had a very full day.'

'SHOs aren't allowed to be tired. And being with you is a tonic.'

He reached to take her hand, she liked that. She felt a bit lost, not sure where she was with him, what exactly their relationship was. And she felt that he had the same kind of doubts. After all, they didn't know each other very well.

There were people walking down a path close to them, laughing and chattering. 'They're going for the last hour at the Red Lion,' she said.

'Where we met less than a week ago.'

Lucy nodded. 'I remember it well. You've had a big effect on me.'

She knew she was revealing herself, making herself vulnerable, by saying such a thing. This was not like the old, tough, Lucy. But what she had said was true. She had to admit it.

He squeezed her hand again. They paced on for a few more steps and then he said, 'I guess I feel the same way. And I wouldn't want it any other way, although it's frightening. We ought to be just a couple of medical people who have met, like each other and are seeing each other, wondering what will develop. But it's more than that, isn't it?'

'I suppose it is.' She thought about their last meeting, when they had been on their way to have dinner. She wanted to stay as they were, happy in each other's company. But there was something that was worrying her. 'Last time we met you said there were things that we had to talk about. What things?'

He sighed. 'Perhaps so. If I am to be honourable, there are things that you should know about me. Things that might affect your view of me.'

Honourable? She didn't like the word. All sorts of

unpleasant possibilities swirled in her mind. One above all. 'So there is another woman?'

He laughed, shook his head. 'Nothing at all like that. I will explain. But first, are you hungry?'

It had never crossed her mind. But now that he had asked, she realised that she had eaten nothing for eight hours but two bars of chocolate, washed down by several cups of coffee. 'Yes, I'm hungry,' she said.

'Then would you like to come to my flat for a meal? Nothing much exciting, perhaps an omelette and salad. And a glass of wine.'

'Sounds perfect. Are you a good cook?'

'I have learned to cope. I can even cook English chips—medical students cannot exist without chips. I'm afraid my flat is as dingy as ever, I am still hoping to take you up on your offer to help me turn it into a home. But, for tonight, you being there will light it up. And then we'll talk.'

He squeezed her hand yet again. 'I do like being with you, Lucy. And I have missed you so much.'

A quick remark, but how it made her heart beat!

So she sat in the corner of his tiny kitchen and watched the deft way he cooked—lighting the oven to finish the half-cooked rolls, tearing the salad, mixing the dressing, beating the eggs.

It was good to watch his movements. He became absorbed in what he was doing, trying to get everything just right.

'Have you ever thought of training to be a surgeon?' she asked.

He smiled at her. 'No. Why?'

'You work with such speed and precision. I can do

everything you've done but it would take me twice as long.'

'I doubt that. A midwife needs speed and precision, too. Look how small and slippery newborn babies are.'

She laughed. 'Perhaps so. But you'd be a good surgeon.'

For some reason his face became blank. 'I'm going to be a generalist, a GP,' he said. 'Though if I had my own way, I would like to specialise in obs and gynae.'

Before she could ask him more about this, why he couldn't have his own way, he said, 'But now I think we are ready. Shall we dine?'

Carrying a tray, he led her into the living room. He unfolded a small table, set it quickly and arranged two chairs. Then he fetched glasses and a bottle of wine from the fridge.

Lucy had thought they might eat off their knees in the living room. That's what she would have done in the nurses' home. But sitting formally at the table was infinitely preferable. It turned the meal into an occasion. And she was enjoying herself—especially when she tasted the white wine he had poured her. If there were troubles to deal with, they could wait.

'So how was the course in London?' she asked.

'Very hard work but very impressive. I'll be a better doctor because of it. I must thank John for sending me on it.'

'So was going on it worth missing our dinner date?' she asked with a smile.

'If I were asked which would give me greater pleasure, then no contest, it would be dinner with you. But life isn't always about pleasure. Now, more wine?'

It was a simple but superb meal. And when he was finished he said he would fetch coffee. Perhaps she would like a liqueur?

'That would be wonderful,' she said. She looked at his face again, saw the fatigue there. 'But on one condition. You let me wash up.'

'Lucy, there is no need. I—'

'Or I'll go now,' she threatened.

So she washed the few dishes while he percolated the coffee, fetched a green bottle and two tiny glasses out of a cupboard. Then they went back to the living room, and this time sat companionably on the couch.

She sipped the green liqueur in the tiny glass and turned to him, her eyebrows raised in shock. 'Marc! What *is* this?'

'It's a liqueur that is native to the countryside where I live. More than sixty local herbs go to make that drink and the alcohol level is very high. My countrymen believe that it is a *restoratif*.'

'It's certainly restoring me. Now, Marc, what do you have to tell me? What's so important that you hinted about?'

He didn't answer quite at once. Instead he said, 'I did enjoy being with your sisters and your family on Saturday. You are obviously all very close.'

'They're my life,' she said.

'So I see. I understand and I envy you. I have no brothers or sisters—not now.'

She was about to ask about why when he rose to his feet and fetched a letter from a small desk.

'You ask what I have to tell you that is so important,' he said. 'I will give you an indication. My mother writes to me at least once a week, we have to keep in touch. I will translate some of her letter, it might give you an idea of her character.'

Lucy thought it an odd thing to do, to read his mother's letter to show what was important. But whatever he thought fit.

'"Melanie d'Ancourt came to dinner last night with her parents, and asked carefully after you. She is now a lawyer, doing very well. She asked if you would call on her next time you are home. In fact, I will invite her to dinner. It is time you were married and settled down, and Melanie would be very suitable".'

'Is she suitable?' asked Lucy.

'Very suitable. A man could be proud of a wife like that. She knows or is related to every notable family in the valley.' He grinned. 'And I can't stand her. She is the kind of woman who wouldn't let you kiss her if she had just put her lipstick on.'

Lucy laughed—slightly because of relief. Then she asked, 'Does your mother try to organise your life? And you put up with it?'

'Things—especially in our rather old-fashioned bit of France—tend to be different from this country.'

'I'm fascinated. But I can't quite make out why you're telling me this.'

'It is hard to describe. There is a saying in my valley: "Every man marries two women—his wife and his land". And eventually I will have to go home, to my land, my second marriage. It is my duty.'

'So what are you saying? That anything between us will only end in sending Christmas cards?'

'No! I wish to...I look forward to...to seeing you,

getting to know you. You are the most surprising, the most wonderful thing that has ever happened to me. But I must warn you. I am not a free man. In time I will go back to Montreval. And I know you would not be happy there. Whatever happens, when I go back, things between us must end.'

He had said it. As simply and as brutally as that.

She had never done anything quite as forward. She leaned forward, gently put her hand over his mouth. 'Marc, you have one big fault!'

He looked confused. 'I have?'

'Yes. You're talking too much. You're worrying too much. All we have to do now is just get on with our jobs and, if we want, see each other. We'll wait and see how our lives go—live in the present, not the future.'

He frowned. 'Is it that simple?'

'It's that simple. And you could start living in the present by kissing me again.'

Perhaps there had been too much talk of emotion as the kiss turned out to be a friendly one. They sat side by side on the couch, their arms round each other and kissed. In time more would come, that was understood. But for the moment this was bliss.

'That was very nice,' she murmured, and pulled his head onto her shoulder. And two minutes later he was asleep.

'Didn't think that sleeping with him would be quite like this,' she muttered, but it was so comfortable there that she also closed her eyes. Just for a moment, she thought. But when she opened them, it was one o'clock in the morning.

Something had disturbed her. Marc had said something. And then, in his sleep, he spoke again. 'Simone,' he muttered, 'Simone.'

Simone was a girl's name. Why was he calling out a girl's name in his sleep?

Carefully, she tried to disentangle herself but he woke anyway.

'Lucy? I'm sorry, I must have fallen asleep.'

'It doesn't matter. I have to go home now anyway.'

Even though he had just woken up, he was alert. 'Lucy, your voice has changed. Something has upset you? What is wrong?'

'You were talking in your sleep. Who is Simone?'

She did not get the reaction she had expected. He laughed. 'And you wondered who she was, what she was to me? Simone is a young, very attractive French girl. She is also my cousin and has been a problem to me and to the rest of my family since she was born. She's just come to England, my mother wrote about her in her letter. Would you like me to read—?'

'No! Marc, I'm so sorry, you must think me… But I still think I ought to be going home now.'

He looked at her, his eyes still sleepy. 'You could always stay and…'

She shook her head. 'Some time perhaps. Not yet.'

'Perhaps so. Now, I shall walk you back to the nurses' home.'

'You're tired, there's no need, it's only five minutes' walk.'

He stood, offered his hands to help her to stand, too. 'You know I'm going to walk you home, don't you?' he asked. 'And I'm doing it because I want to.'

So they walked to the nurses' home, holding hands. Outside, he kissed her again. 'You know I'm looking forward to living in our present,' he said. 'Our present, not our future.'

'Our present, not our future,' she said. 'I'll hold you to that.'

It was only ten minutes before Lucy was in bed. But before she went to sleep she thought of what Marc had told her. He had been honourable. He had said that in time he would have to return to his home, and that he did not think she would be happy there. That when that time came, things between them must end.

Well, they would see. This was a battle between her and a tiny place in the south-east of France. And it was a battle she intended to win.

CHAPTER FOUR

THE next day both were working normal shifts and they had agreed to meet in the evening. So she was surprised—though pleased—when he came onto her ward just after the nurses had finished serving tea.

'The registrar asked me if I'd come to have a quick word with Astrid Duplessis,' he explained. 'More a social visit than a medical one. I gather he hasn't discharged her yet.'

'He's a bit worried about her being lonely and looking after herself in a bedsit,' Lucy said. 'And we still don't know much about her. He's informed Social Services.'

'I may have some news for her. Lucy, may we talk in private for a moment? I think I need your opinion.'

Good to be asked, Lucy thought as she led him to the now empty doctor's room.

'France isn't like England,' he said when they were sitting together. 'In most towns the mayor has far more power than could be dreamed of by an English mayor. And he tends to know many of his townspeople.'

'Go on,' said Lucy. 'Marc, I've a nasty suspicion you've been cutting corners.'

'Possibly. I phoned the mayor of Astrid's home town. Obviously I am French, I explained that I was a doctor in England and that I was interested in a young Englishman who had stayed in a hostel in the town a few months ago. I said we needed to trace his whereabouts but I couldn't say why. The mayor said that he would make enquiries. He rang me back two hours later with the address of a Kevin Connolly, in this town. It was on record in the gendarmerie.'

'Why couldn't Astrid get his address that way?'

Marc shrugged. 'Because she was an eighteen-year-old-girl and not a doctor. Or perhaps she just didn't think.'

'So what have you done with this address?'

'I don't know whether to give it to Social Services or to Astrid or to go and see Kevin myself. If he's still there.'

'You can't just give it to Astrid,' Lucy said. 'She's in no fit state to handle any more disappointment.'

'Why should there necessarily be disappointment?'

Lucy looked at him, a wry smile on her lips. 'Come on, Marc! A quick holiday romance that happened months ago? What man is going to want to discover that he's going to be a father?'

'Perhaps they were—or are—genuinely in love. Perhaps Kevin will be pleased to be re-united with Astrid.'

Lucy shook her head and sighed. 'Marc, I thought I was bad, but it's you who is one of the world's great romantics. And you need to be a realist. Now, go and chat to Astrid for ten minutes but don't tell her what you've found out. And when we've finished work we'll go together to see this Kevin.'

'An admirable idea,' he said.

Three hours later they were standing outside the door of a neat semi on the outskirts of the city. They had driven in Lucy's car, it was handiest. Now she turned to look at him. 'Still think this is a good idea?'

'What's written on that chain round your neck, Lucy?'

She fingered the gold chain, the present from her parents. 'I told you once,' she said. 'It's Latin for love conquers all.'

'Let's hope that is true.' He knocked at the door.

The door was opened by a pleasant-looking young man, wearing a blue and white striped apron. 'Mr Kevin Connolly?' Marc asked.

'The very same. Sorry for the messy outfit, I'm doing a bit of cooking. And I'm afraid my parents are out. How can I help you?'

It was Lucy's turn to speak. 'Do you know an Astrid Duplessis?'

There was shock, and then a great smile spread over the lad's face. 'Astrid! Do you know where she is? Does she want to see me?'

'You might say that,' said Lucy. 'May we come in?'

It was dark by the time they drove back into the hospital grounds. Lucy pulled into her parking slot, turned to look at Marc. 'Are we pleased with our evening's work?' she asked. 'Have we done right?'

He moved his hands in an expressive, entirely French gesture. 'I do not know. Astrid is our patient, her interests must come first. Perhaps re-uniting her with Kevin is a good thing. I think so. He seemed so pleased to hear that she had not abandoned him, that she still loved him.'

'He looked horrified when he heard he was about to become a father.'

'That is true. Though he accepted the idea.' He mused a moment. 'Sometimes, when things happen to you, to your family…it is necessary to grow up quickly. And it can hurt.'

Lucy wondered what he meant by that, but decided not to ask him—not yet. She said, 'I'd rather Astrid was re-united with her parents than with Kevin. Even though I liked the lad. Her parents will be more use to her than Kevin will.'

'Lucy! The boy is in love with her! He'll do everything he can for her.'

'He might now. We'll see what happens in the future.'

'I thought Kevin showed something nearly as important as love. He showed a sense of duty, of responsibility. After the first shock he showed resilience, I would trust him with Astrid.'

'I really hope you're right,' Lucy said.

They climbed out of the car. 'I am not ready to go to bed,' he said, 'I'm too wound up. For a few minutes I'd like to walk through the grounds. Will you accompany me?'

'Of course,' she said. 'You know what, Marc? It's good to have time to ourselves.'

'Midwives, nurses, doctors—they're always needed by other people,' he said. 'That's both the disadvantage and the advantage of the job.'

'Very true.'

So they walked slowly through the dark grounds. It was still warm, the night smelt of earth, of plants. He took her hand, squeezed it. 'This is relaxing, so pleasant,' he said.

She was enjoying just being with him, enjoying his

company, talking casually of nothing very much. And after twenty minutes they were outside the nurses' home. She was enjoying being with him.. but, still, she yawned.

They slowed, stood facing each other. They were in the shadow of a great lime tree, the night was filled with the scent of it. He put his arms round her to kiss her. She wanted him to kiss her properly. Half-fearfully, she expected it. A true kiss was something special. It was a declaration. And when his arms slid round her she sighed.

They were so close together, their bodies touching at thigh and hip, her breasts pressed against the muscles of his chest. He held her gently, but she could sense the latent power in his arms. Though the cotton of her T-shirt she felt his fingertips caress her back.

And he kissed her. She had never felt like this before. She lost all sense of time and place, knew only that he was kissing her and that she could stay here for ever with him. She felt his body, warm, excited and exciting. And her own body felt pliant, as if whatever he wanted he could have. And this just from one kiss!

In time he released her from whatever it was that had been gripping her, put his hands on her shoulders and gently shook her. She opened her eyes, gave a tiny disappointed cry.

'You should go,' he said. 'You are tired.'

She could tell from his voice that this was as hard for him as it was for her.

She couldn't help herself. She whispered, 'I don't want to go.'

Quickly, he kissed her again. 'But you must. Don't worry, we will meet again soon.'

He eased her away from him, she pulled his head down and snatched one last kiss. 'You're so good to me,' she said, knowing how feeble that sounded. 'Goodnight, Marc.'

She turned, to walk quickly to the front door. If she moved slowly she might think again, perhaps turn back and invite him in for a nightcap. Better move quickly. At the door she turned again, she knew that he would wait until she was inside. He raised a hand to say goodbye, she waved back. Then she went inside.

Her body was still tired but now her thoughts were in turmoil. She undressed, showered, made the ritual mug of cocoa and sat on the bed. Perhaps if she was sensible for a minute or two, considered things rationally, she'd be able to sleep. What about Marc Duvallier?

The first fact was all too obvious. Since she had first met the man she had known that she was drawn to him by a force that she just couldn't explain. And she felt—she knew!—that he felt the same way. Though he'd been a bit slow to admit it.

And never before had a simple goodnight kiss had such an effect on her. Her body, her entire being had responded to him. And she knew without doubt that he had responded to her.

But now was the time to try to be cool, logical. If she could. She felt she had been drawn into something that would be impossible to escape. Not that she wanted to escape.

She calculated, she had only known Marc about a

week. Today had been their first real kiss. He was one of the best-looking, most attractive men she had ever met. She thought they shared a lot. They fitted well together.

So what was it that was now worrying her? Was it because he was foreign? She didn't think so. There were times when his slight French accent, his different way of doing things, even his different way of thinking—they made him madly attractive.

She had to face it. She had fallen for him.

Next morning Lucy went into the ward, half hopeful, half anxious. She wanted to be present when Kevin came in to see Astrid. He had wanted to go to the hospital the previous night but had been persuaded not to by the fact that she needed to rest.

She was waiting when Marc arrived. Very properly, he had told John what they had done. 'What did he say?' Lucy asked.

'He said that if it worked out, it would be an ideal solution to Astrid's situation. You know he believes every baby needs a present father as well as a mother. And your friend Jenny was there. She said that she thought it was all romantic and lovely.'

'Jenny's a romantic,' said Lucy. 'Now, I've arranged things with Sister and I've got my uniform on. I'm just going to check Astrid before she gets a shock. You go and talk to the young lover over there.'

She had just seen a nervous Kevin peer into the ward. In his arms was the largest bunch of roses she had ever seen.

Physically, Astrid was fine, ready to be discharged. Mentally—well… Lucy smiled. That might all change in a moment. 'I've got a surprise for you, Astrid,' she said.

She came out and waved to Kevin. Kevin came bounding down the ward, excitement and apprehension on his face. He disappeared through the curtains. Everyone in the ward heard the shriek of joy. 'Kevin!'

'Well, we've pleased someone this morning,' Lucy said to Marc, who had strolled down the ward. 'And I do—I really do—hope that it'll last.'

'Don't be too cynical. I've just had a word with him. Last night he told his parents what had happened. His mother's a French teacher, by the way. They're shocked but rallying round. They're going to ask Astrid if she'd like to stay with them, for as long as she likes. Certainly until after the baby is born.'

He took her arm, looked at her thoughtfully. 'Happy endings are possible, Lucy.'

'Then I want one,' she said.

Lucy had asked Marc if he could call in to speak to her just after handover, and here he was. 'I know you're working late tonight,' she told him, 'and you will be for the next couple of days. But I've got an idea.'

He looked at her with smiling suspicion. 'Lucy Stephens, you have that innocent look that means you're plotting something.'

'Me? Plot? Never!' But to herself she thought with some satisfaction, He's getting to know me.

'This evening I'm going to babysit for Lizzie, her husband is taking her to dinner to celebrate their wedding anniversary,' she told him. 'But then I'm off work for three days. I've nothing special to do and I know you're very busy. So just look at these colour samples. Which do you like best?' She handed him a card.

He looked at the samples, then looked at her. 'Why am I looking at colours, Lucy?'

'You said you wanted to do something about your dingy flat. I had a look at the walls when I was there the other night, they're pretty sound. There's decorating gear stored at Lizzie's. I calculate that it'll only take me a day to put a couple of coats of emulsion on the walls and ceiling of the hall and living room.'

He looked at her in amazement. 'You'll do what?'

'I'm an expert decorator,' she told him. 'Well, I'm a good amateur at painting and wallpapering. Our family has always done its own decorating.'

'C'est impossible!' She had noticed that when he was excited he tended to revert to French. 'Lucy, I cannot possibly permit you to… If anyone should do it then I…'

'If a male friend offered to do it, would you accept?'

He had to think, and then she knew he'd answer honestly. 'Yes,' he said, 'but that would be different.'

'Don't I mean as much to you as a male friend?'

He shook his head in disbelief. 'You know you do. I have never met anyone like you.'

'Well, that's lovely. Now, I thought perhaps this primrose for your living room walls and a white with a hint of gold for the hall.'

'Who am I to object?' he said.

'Then I'll be at your front door at eight tomorrow morning. I'll buy the paint on my way to Lizzie's to-night.'

* * *

The aluminium ladder was tied to her car roof, the cleaning materials, brushes, paint-spattered dustsheets all in her boot. And she was wearing her overalls and hat. Marc looked at her in dismay as she bustled past him. 'I didn't quite believe you'd come,' he said.

He looked particularly attractive in his white shirt, as yet without a tie, and his formal trousers.

'I've come. Now, the furniture here is so light that there'll be no problem shifting it. I don't need you so you get off to work and see what things are like when you return.'

He shrugged a Gallic shrug and did as he was told.

Lucy loved decorating. Sometimes being a midwife was hard physical work, but this was different. It didn't take long to shift the furniture to the centre of the room, spread out her sheets and then start the essential preliminary cleaning. The actual painting was the reward.

She worked through the day, stopping for her sandwiches at lunchtime. She was doing well. And then at five o'clock, Marc phoned. 'Lucy, I have to stay at work. I had intended to take you to dinner or cook for you myself, but we have a couple of emergencies here and I just can't get away. Please, don't work longer, go home and rest. Whatever needs to be done can be done later.'

'You don't know me all that well, do you? Carry on with the medical work, Doctor.' And she rang off.

Three quarters of an hour later there was a knock on the door. She slid down her ladder, went to open it. There was a cheerful pizza delivery lad, carrying a flat box. 'It's been paid for,' he said, 'and there's a message I don't understand. It says, ''This is just for the blood sugar''.'

'I understand,' Lucy said with a smile. And the pizza was fine.

Marc finally came in at nine that night. The work was finished—just. And she was sitting in the kitchen, feeling exhausted and happy.

'I did the kitchen ceiling as well,' she said.

He walked around the living room, admired the hall. 'Lucy, you have worked wonders,' he said. shaking his head. Then he came close to her, peered into her eyes. 'And now you are exhausted,' he added.

She had to agree. 'A bit tired.'

'Then you must sleep. But first something to help you rest. Chocolate?'

'That would be wonderful.'

She enjoyed her cocoa every night, was expecting something like that. But the drink he brought her was very different from cocoa. 'Where did you get this?' she gasped. 'It's wonderful.'

'It comes from the West Indies, it's imported specially.' He reached for a bottle, held it over her mug. 'Try a little brandy with it—it adds spice.'

'Well, new experiences. Thank you,' she said.

Then a vast fatigue enveloped her, and she knew that if she didn't sleep soon she would just fall over.

Marc recognised her state. 'You will stay here the night,' he said. 'You will have my bed and I shall sleep on the couch. Please, no arguments.' He walked out of the room, came back with a pile of bedding which he dropped on the couch. He offered her something in white cotton and said with a grin, 'I wasn't expecting a lady visitor overnight, so all I can offer you to sleep in is this T-shirt. The bath is running for you—I think a bath will be better than a shower to-night. There are fresh towels in the bathroom and a new toothbrush. I have changed the bed sheets, there is a glass of water by your bedside. So I will leave you to go to bed. Goodnight, Lucy.'

She stood, went to him, put her arms round his neck and kissed him on the lips. She said, 'This isn't sexual. It's just because you're you.'

He put his arms round her, for a moment pulled her to him. Then he said, 'It's been a long day. Sleep well, Lucy.'

Somehow she dragged herself to the bedroom, dropped her clothes where they fell. She made sure she did not fall asleep in the bath—though it was bliss-ful. When she came out she wrapped a towel round herself to walk to the bedroom. But she paused outside the closed living-room door. Should she go in and…? She thought not.

She groaned as she climbed into the double bed, it was so comfortable. She had so much to think about. And a minute later she was asleep.

Marc poured himself a small glass of brandy. He lis-tened to make sure that Lucy didn't fall asleep in the bath. He had done that himself before. Then he heard her get out, pad along the corridor. He heard her foot-steps stop outside the door. He remained perfectly still. Then the footsteps carried on and he heard the bed-room door shut.

With a sigh he breathed out—how long had he been holding his breath? What would he have done if she had walked into the living room dressed just in a towel? He supposed he was glad she had walked on. Tonight she was vulnerable and it wouldn't have been fair to… But he wanted her so much. He took a mouthful of brandy, coughed and spluttered. He had taken too much.

But the smooth spirit revived him. He had to think about Lucy. He hadn't known her long, only a few days really. He knew that this was a new job, in a new place, meeting new people, learning new techniques. To a certain extent he was bound to be over-wrought. But Lucy had made an impression on him greater than anyone or anything else.

As he had told her, he had had girlfriends before, of course. More than a few. But he had been training and apart from one disaster his affairs had been largely casual, having to fit around work. He was still working. Would he have to fit Lucy around work? Would an affair with Lucy also be casual? He knew that it would not.

He thought she quite…liked him. But she was so different to him! She had many friends, loved being among people. Her life was so different from what his future life was likely to be.

Until now he had been more than content with the idea of his future life, had been looking forward to it.

Perhaps it would be best to keep her as a friend. Or… A cold idea threw him into a panic. For her sake perhaps it would be better to cool off any relationship. If there was to be one. It might be the kindest thing to do, the most honourable thing to do.

But he didn't want to. He needed to see more of Lucy Stephens. Irritated, he went to bed.

*　　*　　*

It was the smell that woke her, a smell of coffee, but coffee such as she'd never had before. Then there was a knock on the door. She pulled the sheet up to her chin and shouted, 'Come in.'

In came Marc, dressed in light-coloured trousers and polo shirt. He looked fresh and alert, obviously already showered and shaved. The very sight of him made her feel excited and uneasy at the same time.

He placed a tray by the bed. On it was a cafetière of coffee, a mug and a jug of hot milk. And there was an extra smell—toast. He said, 'The best of French and English cuisine. French coffee. But no *boulangerie* nearby for fresh croissants, so I've made wholemeal toast and marmalade.'

'Marc, this is fantastic! Breakfast in bed! I've not had that for years.' She thought for a moment. 'Are you having coffee, too?'

'Mine is in the living room.'

'Well, fetch it and sit on the bed and talk to me. That's what my sisters used to do when I was a little girl.'

'My feelings for you are very different from your sisters' feelings.'

She turned rather pink. 'Well, yes. But when I get up I'll be running around like mad. There's lots to do. So a few minutes talking to you will be calming. Sort of,' she added after a moment.

He fetched his coffee and she felt slightly excited when he sat on the bed, and she felt it give way under her. 'Marc, you're so good to me.'

He shook his head. 'No more than you were to me.' He grinned. 'And are you going to worry about my reputation if you're seen leaving my flat?'

She remembered what she had said before, and winced. Then she sighed. 'Who cares?' she asked.

'Who cares indeed?' He drank some coffee.

'It strikes me that now you know an awful lot about me and I don't know much about you. I want to know about your family.'

He nodded. 'And you shall. But it's much smaller than yours. The closest relation is my mother. The family home is in a tiny village high in the French Alps, miles from anywhere. Then there are assorted cousins, uncles, aunts and so on, but they all live quite some distance away. Different from you in this big city.'

'So you're an only child?'

He frowned. 'I am. I had an older brother, he was killed in an accident. But now I am head of the family.'

'Marc, I'm so sorry!'

He shrugged. 'These things happen. But it was hard on us all.' He stood. 'There's a lot more to tell, but now I think I must leave and let you get dressed. I see that last night you undressed in something of a hurry.'

She leaned out of bed, had to blush when she saw her eminently sensible white underwear lying where she had dropped them. 'Well, I was tired,' she said.

'So you were, Now, I'm working today but I have tomorrow off. And so do you.'

'That's right.'

'I could do with some help. Tomorrow, if you wish, perhaps you'd like to spend the day with me. I have to give a lecture to my old school on training to be a doctor. I have been asked if I could also bring a female speaker and there is no one I can think of that would do the job better than you. Could you talk about the work of a midwife?'

'Yes,' said Lucy, after a pause.

'Good. But we'll need to set off quite early. We're going to the Lake District.'

'You went to school in the Lake District?'

'It's where I learned to be what I am. Now, I must go, but before I leave I would like…'

She reached our her arms, pulled him towards her. 'And I want to kiss you, too,' she said.

CHAPTER FIVE

IT WAS going to be a fine day. Good. Lucy felt happy anticipating the trip, this would be the longest she had ever spent alone with Marc. She might find out more about him.

She put on a pretty blue dress, neither too formal nor too casual. Of course, she would take a coat, this was the Lake District. And, most important, she had her notes ready.

As she waited for him, she felt that this day might be different. There might be an alteration in the way he felt. He might waver. She just didn't know.

She hadn't seen his car before. It was a large, black, four-wheel-drive Mercedes, standing high off the ground.

'This is a surprise, it's not an obvious doctor's car,' she said as he helped her into the passenger seat.

'In France I often have to drive long distances. And in the winter you often need the power. May I say how attractive you look?'

'Thank you, kind sir. And you look like every mother's idea of the ideal man for her daughter. Like an overgrown schoolboy, in fact.' Then she reddened. 'I hope you didn't take that too personally.'

He was dressed in blazer, shining white shirt and immaculate grey trousers. There was some kind of official tie that she didn't recognise. He grinned. 'I will take it as a compliment.'

* * *

They took the M6 north. When they were surrounded by hills, they turned off to wriggle along smaller roads and eventually came to a Victorian building. 'Drake College,' he said, 'where I was at school. It specialises in educating the children of parents who have to work for long periods abroad. Especially parents in the armed services.'

She couldn't help herself. 'A child belongs with its parents. Why have children if you're going to send them away?'

'A question I've often asked myself. The answer must be that they thought that it was their duty to work where they couldn't take their children.'

They were now passing the sign saying 'Drake College' and she noticed that underneath, in smaller letters, was another word. '"Service",' she read aloud. 'That's a fine motto for a boarding school. I'd like to have a school where the motto was "Love".'

'Quite a good idea,' he said.

They drove on slowly and in silence for a moment, then she said, 'Sorry. Why am I taking it out on you when it's probably not your fault?'

'I like it when you say what you think. It's an honesty that's quite rare.'

She was rather pleased with this compliment.

He looked thoughtfully over the playing fields. 'I certainly learned a lot here and I wasn't unhappy. The staff were very good. I've got happy memories of being here.'

'Your family must be rich to have sent you here.' She was still irritated by the place.

He shrugged. 'In fact, I won a scholarship. But the

family wouldn't let me take it up. They thought the scholarship should go to someone who really needed the money.'

'So you are rich?'

It seemed to be a new idea to him. 'I suppose I am,' he said. 'But being rich can bring responsibilities.'

'I'd like to have the chance to find out.'

They parked at the front of the school. Marc led her along bewildering corridors and eventually knocked at a study door.

'Enter,' a voice boomed.

Marc winked at Lucy and opened the door.

At first Lucy found it difficult not to laugh. Dr Atkins looked so much like a caricature of a head-master. He was tall, but thin and stooped. He had a halo of white hair, a beaked nose, half-moon glasses. He wore a dark suit and an academic gown.

'Dr Duvallier—Marc! So good to see you again.' Even the voice played the part—it was clear, rather fruity, Lucy thought. He offered his hand to Marc and then said, 'And who might this be?'

'A colleague, Miss Stephens. She is a midwife.'

'Excellent! A male and a female speaker. As ever, Marc, you have done what was asked of you. That will please us all. Now, Miss Stephens, I'll get one of our girls to take you somewhere where you can freshen up. Then perhaps we can begin.'

'Good,' said Lucy.

Why had she offered to give a talk? she wondered as she dabbed water onto her face. It wasn't something she'd done often before. Certainly not at a place like this. But then she realised what the answer was. She had to fight back, to prove herself to Marc. Even though the very idea terrified her.

She had never heard Marc speak in public before, but she'd guessed he'd be good, and he was. They had a mixed audience of about a hundred and twenty, and the students looked alert. Many of them were ready to take notes.

Marc started with a couple of reminiscences about his time at the school and then moved easily into why he had wanted to train to be a doctor. He talked about how to apply, what qualities medicine needed. More importantly, he told them what to expect, how being a doctor was the very opposite of being glamorous. It was more often hard, wearying, boring. But the rewards, when they came, were great.

Then—which pleased Lucy—he pointed out that there were a number of other medical careers which were just as valuable, which could be just as rewarding.

He got a great round of applause. Then he answered questions and got even more applause.

'And now I'd like to introduce Miss Stephens. Miss Stephens is a midwife, she'll tell you a little about her work and then answer questions.'

It was now her turn. Lucy felt like panicking. How could she follow a talk like Marc's? She had said she'd give a talk because she wanted to fight her corner. It wasn't her way to sit quietly and be the humble little assistant. But now she was realising that this might be harder than she had thought.

She stood, looked at the array of interested faces in front of her. This couldn't be harder than the first time she had delivered a baby. She took two deep breaths, and smiled. She'd decided to add to her prepared speech.

'We're in a room in the delivery suite,' she said. 'I'm the midwife, I'm in charge, though I have an assistant. If I need a doctor then I send for one. I've got a mother sweating and moaning on the bed. By her head is her husband, he's holding her hand and occasionally wiping her face. It's their first child and he's more worried than his wife.

'She's been in labour for eight hours now and is well into the second stage. She's been pushing desperately for over an hour, she's in pain and she's more tired than she has ever been in her life before. But that is fine. Everything is going according to plan. It's going to be a nice straightforward birth, like the other three I've supervised this week. Just another working day.'

Lucy paused, sipped from her glass of water. 'But you must never forget, for the mother it isn't just another working day. For her, this is one of the most important, most memorable days of her life.

'The mother is sitting up, propped up by pillows. Her legs are drawn up, knees spread wide apart. I examine her, see a little dark brown hair covered with white grease. It's the baby's head. I tell her to push. She does. Each time she pushes the head comes out a little, then slips back. But it's being born.

'Eventually the head doesn't recede. I tell the mother not to push at the next contraction, but to pant. I put my hand on the baby's head, it mustn't be born in too much of a rush.

'The head comes out and the mother cries out…

screams, in fact. But it's a scream of effort. This is hard work. Quickly, I clean the baby's face, aspirate mucus from its nose and mouth.

'It's not out yet but we don't hurry at this stage. At the next contraction the mother is told to push again. One shoulder emerges. And the baby slowly turns, as they all do as they are being born, and the second shoulder emerges. Then the baby slips into the hands of the assistant whose job it is to take the newborn child.

'And there's the first tiny cry.'

Lucy glanced at her audience. They were rapt. One or two of them even had their mouths open. She went on, 'I tell the mother and father that it's a little girl. And there's a lightning check to make sure there are no obvious problems. There aren't in the great majority of births. Then the baby is wrapped in a warm blanket and put on the breast of the mother. She puts her arm round her new child and looks down at her. This is hers, her child, created by her and her husband. They've made an entire new person. And that is a magic moment. I have to admit, I've supervised a lot of births but I still find it a magic moment and I often cry myself a bit.'

She stopped, took a deep breath. 'Of course, there's lots of other things to do. There's the cord to be cut, the placenta to be delivered, the baby to be assessed. But the major part of the job is done. And I am happy. And that is why I chose to be a midwife.'

She stopped, and she thought she could feel her audience breathing out. She had held them. It was a good feeling.

'Now…the qualifications you need…' From now on

it was all easy going. Straightforward stuff about training, the various kinds of midwifery, prospects for the
future.

She finished. Another great burst of applause. A tiny
thought of which she was instantly ashamed—she was
clapped even more vigorously than Marc.

'Have you ever thought of being a teacher?' Dr Atkins
asked Lucy as they walked back to his study. 'You'd
be good at it.'

She was going to have tea with the headmaster
alone. Marc had been invited by a few senior boys to
come and see where he used to study. Lucy had been
invited too but she had declined. This ought to be
Marc's visit.

'I'm very happy to be a midwife,' she said. 'But
when I get more experience, I expect I'll be training
junior midwives. I'll enjoy that.'

'I'm sure you will. How long have you known the
Comte de Montreval?'

'Who?' Lucy was bewildered.

Dr Atkins stopped, looked at her thoughtfully. 'He
hasn't told you, I see. Marc is the Comte de
Montreval.'

Lucy felt that she needed time to stop and think
about this. Marc an aristocrat? What else had he kept
from her? She'd told him everything about herself and
her family.

'I didn't realise. But, then, I haven't known him
long.'

'I'm sure he will mention it in time. He finds it both
an honour and a burden. Particularly since his brother
Auguste died…' Dr Atkins's voice trailed away. 'But

I must say, he seemed far more relaxed, happier than the last time I saw him. Things must be going right for him in some respect.'

'I hope so,' Lucy replied, before adding, 'The man is an enigma.'

They set off in early evening, it would be a long drive back. 'What did you think of my old school?' Marc asked when they were well on the motorway.

'Nothing would make me send my children away to school. But if I had to—then I'd send them to a place like that. Has Dr Atkins always been a teacher?'

'No. He got to quite a high rank in the army. In fact he wrote two or three very well thought-of books on strategy and tactics.'

'Really?' said Lucy. She wondered if quite a lot of Dr Atkins had rubbed off on Marc.

He drove on a little further and then said, 'When we get nearer home, would you like to turn off the motorway, find a restaurant somewhere for dinner?'

She considered this. 'Yes, but...do you like Indian food?'

'Very much so. Why?'

'There's a very good Indian take-away near the hospital. I'm tired, you must be too. Why not let's go back to your flat, order a take-away and eat there?'

He seemed puzzled. 'If that's what you want,' he said.

She leaned over to stroke his hand on the wheel. 'I'm tired,' she said. 'You might be used to public speaking, I'm not. So I'm going to put on some mood music and doze.'

'Pull that lever and recline the seat,' he said. 'There's a set of discs there.'

She turned the music low, reclined her seat and tried to relax. At first her thoughts went round and round—what had she learned about Marc, did she feel any different about him? She didn't know, she just couldn't make it all out. And so, quite quickly, she went to sleep.

When she woke up they weren't too far from the hospital. She had slept deeply—and found that she was refreshed and that her mind was made up.

'If you drop me off at my place, I'll change,' she said, 'then walk over to your flat.'

'I'll fetch you.'

'Not that distance you won't. I can walk three hundred yards.'

She had a quick shower, changed into trousers and a shirt. Clothes for idling in. She went into her bathroom, hesitated a minute. Then she took a few things out of the cupboard and put them into her handbag. A decision.

He must have been looking out for her as he opened the door before she could knock. That was nice. He'd changed into jeans and T-shirt. No socks, his feet in old leather moccasins. 'Come in! I hope you're hungry. I've phoned and ordered the banquet for two. It'll come in another half-hour, give us time for a drink first.'

He led her into the living room. She looked around with some pride at her decorating. It had certainly made a difference to the room, the primrose walls made it so much more welcoming.

The small table was set out with glasses and cutlery. 'The plates are warming. I see no reason why we have to eat out of foil containers.'

'True.'

He poured her a glass of dark red wine. As he handed it to her he said, 'Indian food is very spicy. I picked this Rioja—it's oaky, strong enough not to be overwhelmed by the spices.'

She sipped. 'Very nice,' she said.

'And afterwards I will make you some of my own coffee.'

She had to smile. 'Marc, this is just a take-away— even though a very good one. You shouldn't have gone to all this trouble.'

He shook his head, looked serious. 'No. No matter how simple a meal might be, if it is served properly it doubles the pleasure. And this is a banquet—we will treat it as such.'

'I suppose so,' she said. 'And I do like this red wine.'

Shortly afterwards the meal arrived. Marc said he was the host, wouldn't let her into his kitchen. So she had to wait until he brought out the warmed plates, a set of bowls on a chafing dish, a central plate of neatly arranged sambals. Only then could they sit down, shake out the napkins and start to eat.

After a while she asked, 'Is there any French food that you can't get here? Anything that you really miss?'

He thought a moment. 'In the mountains where I come from, there are some regional dishes that I very much miss. There are wild boar hams which are coated in herbs and then dried. There are a number of thick soups or stews, which started as food for the poor, using only what was cheap and local. Often they were cooked for hours. Yes, I miss them.' He grinned. 'And you have already tasted the mountain liqueur, we'll have another later. Now, more wine?'

Because they were sitting at the table, chatting as they ate, the meal took longer than she would have thought. And it was more enjoyable. She realised that this was a man who could change her in some ways. He could make even as simple a thing as eating a meal into something, well, magic.

'You know,' she said, 'never again am I going to eat a meal standing by the kitchen table because I just don't have time to sit down.'

He laughed. 'That's just a dream. You're a midwife, I'm a doctor. Sometimes lack of time means that you have to eat standing up.'

'That's not eating. That's refuelling.'

When they finally finished, she insisted on at least helping him to carry the dishes into the kitchen. But he refused to let her wash up this time. He said that it could wait and to sit down and he would bring her coffee.

They sat side by side on the couch, drank his excellent coffee. And he offered her a small glass filled with the green liquid he had given her before.

They drank coffee and tasted the liqueur. She felt happy sitting there, could have been content just to be there with him, waiting to see what might happen.

But she had made up her mind. In so many ways he was still an enigma to her, there were things he had to tell her. She needed to know him better, felt that their relationship could never progress until things were clearer.

'You've met a lot of my family,' she said. 'You know that we're close. If you're a friend of mine then you're a friend of them all. Now, I want to know more about your family. And I want to know about you and your brother Auguste and why you never told me that you are the Comte de Montreval.'

She could feel the relaxed figure by her side suddenly become taut. His voice tried to remain calm, but she could detect a thread of anger in it. 'How did you know about me being a comte? And Auguste? Did Dr Atkins tell you?'

'He let a little slip. I learned more from him than I have from you.'

Marc took a deep breath, she could feel his chest swelling by her side. Then he let out the breath in a long sigh. 'I try to keep the two halves of my life apart,' he said.

She stretched over to take one of his hands. 'Will you tell me, please?' she said. 'I need to know you and I feel I don't know you yet.'

He took her hand in both of his and she felt his fingers trailing over her palm, caressing gently. Then he lifted the hand and kissed her fingertips. 'First, perhaps there are things I should show you,' he said.

He put her hand down—regretfully, she thought. Then he fetched a folder from his study, put it on the table in front of them. First there was a photograph. 'The castle and village of Montreval,' he said. 'They have belonged to my family for five hundred years or more.'

She looked, fascinated. 'It's like something out of a fairy-tale,' she said.

'Remember that fairy-tales are often quite frightening. Cruel stories. Montreval is both a beautiful and a hard place.'

She looked further. The castle and village were in a narrow valley. The castle was perched on the hillside, a structure of towers and parapets and battlements. Behind the village were steep mountains. There was a scattering of houses, the occasional cultivated field. 'It looks lonely,' she said doubtfully. 'Beautiful but lonely.'

'It is but I love it. Lucy, when the wild flowers come out in spring…' He shook his head. 'You must come and see.'

Then he showed her a map. 'This little wriggling line is the only road into the village. The nearest town is thirty miles away—here, Brouville. In winter we are always cut off by snow.'

He pushed the map away and frowned. 'Montreval hasn't changed in centuries. There is not enough for the young people to do, they have to leave to work in the towns. In many young families, the man works away, sends money home. But no one wishes to leave. They were born there, it is their home.'

'So are you the only one left in your family? There must be others.'

'My father died some years ago. And my older brother Auguste…was killed. At present the estate is run by my mother. She is good at it, likes it. When I return I shall take over her work. But I intend to return to be a doctor. The village and the surrounding farms desperately need one. And I have plans to build a

clinic that will serve the entire area. When I have finished training, I shall go back to Montreval.'

'Are you looking forward to that?'

'Of course. It is my destiny. And who could not
love the countryside there?'

Lucy was struggling with this. 'Do you want to
spend your life in a tiny place like that?'

'Generations of my family have been happy there.
Why should I not be happy?'

'So when do you think you'll go back?'

'I will finish my time in O and G. Then I shall
return.'

Lucy just didn't know what to make of that. It was
a situation she had never come across before.

'Do you get on well with your mother?' she asked.

'Very well. She was the one who sent me away to
boarding school. She wanted the younger member of
the family to be able to leave Montreval, to have the
chance of a completely different life. But then Auguste
was killed and I knew that I had to go back. At present
my life is medicine. But eventually it must be medicine and Montreval.'

'You know what?' Lucy said. 'I've spent too much
time today talking about the higher things in life, and
trying to grasp difficult ideas. I need to get my feet
back on the ground. You won't like this, but this is
what I want. You finish your coffee. I'm going to wash
up.'

'You're what?'

'I'm going to wash up. A simple, ordinary job.
Now, don't start on that I'm your guest or anything,
it's just that I need to get grounded again. And washing up will do it for me.'

He shook his head. 'I don't deserve anyone like you,' he said.

'Just keep out of the kitchen for a while.'

In fact, there wasn't much to do. But the simple tasks helped her to decide exactly what she needed to do. Her mind was made up.

When she had washed up she went to the bathroom, washed her face and cleaned her teeth then returned to the living room. 'I'd like some music on, please,' she said, 'but you choose this time.'

He walked to a rack of discs, thought for a moment then selected one. Lucy sat on the couch again, listened. There was a curious, old-fashioned-sounding orchestra, then a woman started to sing in French. At first she didn't like it, but after a moment or two the plaintive sound seemed quite moving. 'What is it?' she asked.

'"*C'etait une histoire d'amour*". A love story.' He quoted a couple of lines. She loved it when he spoke in French.

He came to sit next to her, she took his hand. Another song, sad again. 'It's called "A young man was singing",' he told her. 'You can probably guess what he is singing about.'

'Who is it? Marc, it's old-fashioned but it's beautiful. Who is it?'

He smiled. 'Wait a minute. There's a bit in English in the next song. And then you'll recognise who it is at once.'

And of course she did. She should have known that throaty voice instantly. 'It's Edith Piaf!' Lucy said. 'A wonderful voice.'

'True. Edith Piaf, the little sparrow. I love listening to her.'

It had been a long day but she was far from tired. He was stroking her hand again, in a way that felt relaxing but gently exciting. He lifted her hand, kissed the fingertips again.

The song ended, and another one started. '''*Je n'en connais le fin*'',' he told her.

'I don't know how it will end,' she translated.

'Very good. And very true.' He leaned over, turned off the CD player. Then he put his arm round her and kissed her, but this time on the lips.

She did not know how this would end. But she knew that this was a beginning and there was no need to hurry.

It was a gentle kiss at first. They were sitting on the couch side by side, he put his arm round her and bent over to kiss her. She lay back, perfectly relaxed, content for the moment just to be there, to be passive and see what might happen. But she knew she wouldn't feel this way for long.

Her senses seemed heightened. She could see nothing, her eyes were closed. But she felt the softness, the smoothness of the couch. She smelt the soap he had used, the lemony aftershave. And under it all she smelt the warmth of him. There was no more Edith Piaf, but outside she could hear the joyous song of a skylark. And taste. She could taste him. As he kissed her.

She wasn't sure how long they stayed like that. Her arms were round him, her fingers in the crisp hair on the back of his neck. She ran her hands down his spine to feel the great columns of muscle on each side. And he leaned further towards her, pulling them closer together.

Her breasts were hard against his chest. And how he was kissing her! Then he stopped, and she opened her eyes. Could see his eyes, so close, the grey now almost black, carrying a message that was unmistakable.

She mumbled, 'I'm lying here, relaxed and very happy, and you're bent over me. You must be cramped, hurting your spine, twisting like that.' Quickly she darted her head forward, kissed him on the lips. Then she jumped to her feet, turned to him, still sitting, and took his hands in hers. She pulled him upright. 'Take me somewhere where we can be comfortable together,' she said.

She had decided. Whatever was to be between them, she wanted to be a willing partner. So she went on, 'And I want to tell you now—whatever happens between us, everything will be safe.'

She hoped this coded message would be enough for him. It was. She could see the delight, the excitement in his eyes now. He wrapped his arms round her and kissed her again. Now their bodies were pressed close she could feel his excitement. And she felt almost weak, as if her bones had turned to water. She wanted him so much.

This again was a different kiss, the kiss of a lover, urgent, demanding. She responded, pressing herself against him, moulding their bodies together. Eventually they broke apart. 'Come to bed,' he said. He took her by the hands and led her.

She had slept in this bed before, had been comfortable there. She had sat up in the bed in the morning, had breakfast with this man. But now the bed looked different.

The curtains were not drawn, it was twilight. He kissed her once more then, with infinite care, pulled her shirt over her head. He reached behind her, unhooked her bra. Then he stepped back.

She stood before him, proud as he looked at her, saw the passion burning even deeper in his eyes. She touched the gold chain, the medallion round her neck. *Amor vincit omnia.* 'I want to keep this on,' she said. And he stooped, kissed the medallion. Then he stooped further, kissed the aching pink tips of her breasts. She gasped with joy.

'Now you,' she muttered, pulling the T-shirt over his head. And then leaned to grasp him to her so that the heat of their skins was joined. Her arms were still round his neck as he felt for the waistband of her trousers and loosened her belt. Then he bent to slide them down to her ankles, taking her thong, too. She felt proud to be naked before him.

And anxious that he be naked too. So she pulled him up, felt for his belt and unsnapped it.

Now they were both naked. He kissed her fiercely, their bodies untrammelled by clothes, and she felt the hardness of his need for her. Then, somehow, they were on the bed together.

He was in charge, pressing her body downwards. He kissed her. His lips roved over her body, down her neck to the still aching peaks of her breasts and then further below to kiss her with that ultimate intimacy that made her back arch and made her call his name out loud in agonised happiness.

Both felt the gathering urgency. He was poised

above her. She drew up her legs, offering her body, herself, to him. She wanted him, needed him, and she had to have him now. She sighed as he drove deep within her. She knew he could feel her warmth and dampness, exciting him. She urged him onwards, thrusting her hips towards him. She wanted Marc to have her…now…now…yes, now! She screamed his name, shaking her head from side to side, pulling him to her and knowing so well that he had reached the same climax as herself.

There was no need for words. No words could tell what they had felt. They lay side by side, the sweat cooling on their heated bodes. He held her hand in his, an arm under her head. She had never felt like this before.

She knew what would happen next. As she lay in his arms she burst into tears. And then she could feel his anguish.

'Sweetheart, what is it? Why are you crying?'

'Don't worry, please, don't worry,' she said. 'I always cry when I'm happy.'

CHAPTER SIX

SHE woke early the next morning. She woke first, knowing she had slept well. There were the birds outside, sunlight probed through the sides of Marc's blinds. Otherwise, the room was dark.

She was resting against the warmth of his naked body. As she brushed herself against his back she felt her nipples come erect and then the rest of her body responded. She had never felt this way before.

It was early, she could see from the clock by his bedside. No need to wake, no need to go to work. But she couldn't sleep again. There was too much to think about.

She thought about the evening before, the rapture she had felt. Then she thought of earlier, of the songs by Edith Piaf. 'I will have no regrets.' Well, she herself had none. She knew she would never forget the night before. It had been simply something else. But where would it lead? Did they have a future together? Marc was not like any other men she had known. But…she thought of the other song by Piaf. 'I don't know how it will end.' She didn't. But there was a growing certainty in her that she wanted to spend more time with this man.

It was too early to think such deep thoughts! She wriggled, yawned and stretched her arms over her head. She had disturbed him and he rolled over. His

97

arm flopped over her—and suddenly his hand was holding her breast. 'You're awake,' she muttered.

'Oh, yes, I'm awake now. Are you?'

'Well, I will be if you keep doing that.' His thumb was caressing her nipple into a hardness that was almost more than she could bear.

'Then I'd better stop,' he said.

To her instant disappointment, he did stop. But then he rolled further towards her, took her breast in his mouth and she sighed with pleasure. 'We've got at least an hour,' she told him.

'So we're going to work together,' she told him afterwards. 'We're on the same ward. But I gather you're on days and I'm on lates. But we'll be in the same place between two o'clock and half past five.'

'Or longer. They get their money's worth out of me. And I love it.'

'I know you do. Now, you get washed and dressed and I'll make you some breakfast. And after you've gone to work, I'll wander back to my own place and then we'll meet on the ward.'

'After last night it'll be odd working with you,' he said. 'Very odd.'

An hour later he was washed, shaved, breakfasted, dressed as a young doctor should be for a day on the wards. Lucy was wearing his dressing-gown, and had to hike it up to stop herself tripping over the hem. But she was looking as lovely in it as she did when she was smartly dressed.

He kissed her goodbye. A long kiss. 'See you in a few hours,' he said.

'I'm looking forward to it already.' Then she kissed him again.

He stopped in the hall to pick up his mail. There was the usual pile of advertising material, which he would skim through later, and a letter from France, in his mother's clear handwriting. He would take it to work and read it later.

The sun was shining. As he walked across the grass towards the main hospital building, Marc felt particularly happy. Last night had been…well, something else. Something he knew he would never forget. As he would never forget Lucy Stephens.

Work was as fascinating as always. There were drug prescriptions to be written up. He was called down the ward to decide if a patient could have more analgesics. There were IV lines to be inserted, a decision to be made as to whether or not to call the consultant. He knew he was learning a lot from the senior midwifes there, always asked their opinions.

The work was time-consuming, but he liked it. It absorbed him. And it stopped him thinking about other things.

One of the mums-to-be found out that he was French. After Marc had written up her observations she asked him about Provence. Her husband was thinking of taking her and the new baby there for a holiday next spring and she was a little nervous.

'You will love it, Mrs Kennedy,' Marc assured her. 'Spring is the very best time to go. The flowers are coming out, it isn't too hot and there aren't too many tourists.'

'But the baby? Will it be all right?'

'The baby will love it. And I can assure you that in

the very unlikely event of you needing medical advice, the French medical service is excellent.'

'Oh, I didn't mean to suggest… I mean, you being French and all, I…'

He patted her shoulder. 'Of course not. Now, you have this baby, and afterwards you can dream of your holiday in Provence. I promise you will enjoy it.'

He knew, of course, that Mrs Kennedy didn't really want to talk about France. She just wanted a little human contact, a little reassurance. The kind of thing that Lucy was so good at. She'd have been pleased with me, dealing with Mrs Kennedy, he thought. And the thought of her being pleased with him pleased him even more.

The morning wore on. It was unusually quiet on the ward, he had plenty of time to go to the doctors' room and sort out his paperwork. He even had time for a long coffee-break. And he shut his eyes and thought of the night before.

The image came back, Lucy in his dressing-gown, kissing him goodbye. They had had breakfast together. Just before that they had made love. Her hair had still been tousled, she had worn no make-up, but the brightness of her eyes and the happiness of her smile had made her lovely. Like a… He had to think it. Like a newly married wife.

She would make a wonderful wife. He had only known her a short time, and yet she'd made such an impression on him. Not only the love-making last night, but the way she talked, thought, tried to make him happy and was always happy herself. He sighed. He had to face it, he had fallen in love with her. He felt more for her than he had felt for any woman in his life before.

In two or three months he thought that he might… might what? Of course, they both might find that the attraction between them was passing, it had happened before. But something told him that it wouldn't happen this time.

He thought about her life. She was a dazzling person, loved being surrounded by people. She wanted— needed—to be close to her family. What was the expression? She was a people person.

As he poured himself another cup of coffee he noticed the letter from his mother sticking out of his pocket. Time to find out what was happening in Montreval. He opened the letter, scanned the details about the estate that his mother always sent.

No really good news. A couple more young men had decided that their work was too hard and their pay too poor and they had gone to the city. The government had sent surveyors round who had spent all their time asking questions, getting in people's way and generally causing unrest. The autumn crops looked as if they would be a little worse than last year. The chateau needed extensive and expensive repairs. So far, so typical—a report, not a letter. Then came the personal details.

I have not wanted to worry you and so have said nothing about this so far. However, after pains in my chest, I was referred to a consultant in Lyons. I enclose his address and if you phone I have asked him to speak to you fully. But his message is simple. I have a heart condition that will in time get worse.

*I must cut down on work. I may stay at home for
the next six months, but after that I must make arrangements to spend my winters somewhere more
hospitable than Montreval. My son, I fear it will
soon be time for you to take up your duties here…*

Marc paled, read and reread the letter. He would
phone the consultant in Lyons that afternoon, but he
knew that it was not in his mother's nature to exag-
gerate. She was ill.

Now there was a definite time for him to return to
Montreval. He had no choice, it was his destiny and
he accepted it. He would leave this hospital next summer…he had perhaps ten more months here.

What was he to do about Lucy? Could she be happy
in Montreval? Would it be fair to ask her to go there?
His future was there, would she wish to share it? It
was so different from the life she might have expected.

He threw down his pen, went down onto the ward
and triple-checked observations that he had double-
checked already.

'I've never been inspected so often,' he was told by
a cheerful mother who had three children already. 'Is
there anything wrong? Anything worrying you?'

'Not a thing, Mrs Jones. I'm just being too careful.
You're absolutely fine.'

Now his private life was making him an inefficient
doctor, he thought. And because he was basically honest, he realised what he was doing. Displacement ac-
tivity. He was working to stop himself thinking.

He looked out of a window, saw the greenness of
the trees. Somewhere out there, either at his flat or her

room, was Lucy. She might be thinking of him. As he was thinking of her.

Fortunately, work on the ward suddenly became more intensive, there was no time for thinking. But later on he was alone in the doctors' room, looking for the tiny glass phials of sodium chloride that were used to flush out the IV tubes.

Smiling, he thought of Lucy. Vaguely, he heard a crack but he paid it no attention. And then, suddenly, he realised that his hand hurt. He looked down and blood was running from between his fingers.

Unknowingly he had squeezed the phial too hard and had broken it. Not too much of a problem. He could get more sodium chloride and it wasn't poisonous.

He washed his fingers, found himself some sticking plaster. He had been told that in hospital every accident, no matter how small, should be written up in the accident book. Not this one. Cause of accident? Being in love? Forget it.

And then it struck him, almost unexpectedly. His mouth opened with the shock of it. But he knew it was right.

His affair with Lucy must end. Perhaps because, for the first time in his life, he was serious about a woman.

And he would have to act now, while he still had the strength of mind.

It was nearly lunchtime. Lucy would be coming onto the ward in a couple of hours. He just couldn't meet her. He phoned one of his fellow SHOs and asked him if he'd finish this shift. In return Marc would work the next Saturday afternoon, when there was an important football match on. Of course, his friend was delighted.

'What's the problem, Marc? Nothing too serious, I hope?'

'Just had a letter from home. A couple of things I have to arrange. Thanks for coming in.'

Then he left word for Lucy with the ward sister that he had been called away and would see her at the end of the shift.

His friend arrived and Marc left. He seemed to be moving with more and more speed towards a disaster that he was causing. And there was nothing he could do.

First he drove out of the hospital grounds. No way did he want to run into Lucy until he was ready. He stopped at a telephone booth and phoned the consultant in Lyons. The conversation went exactly as he had suspected it would.

'Your mother is strong *m'sieur*, but like all of us she is getting old. And Montreval is not a good place to spend a winter when you have a diseased heart. I have given her drugs, told her to work less hard. There is no great need to worry at present. But I feel that the coming winter must be the last in the chateau. A house somewhere on the coast would be much more suitable.'

'Thank you, *m'sieur le docteur*. I will see that that is provided.'

He drove on a little way and parked, and found himself near the park where he had met Lucy and her family. It was only a couple of weeks ago, but so much seemed to have happened since. He remembered how glorious she had seemed, sitting there with the baby on her lap. He remembered how happy she had been with her family. He remembered how happy she had made him.

He sat under the same tree to think. What did he have to do? Was there any way out?

Montreval had to be his first priority. That was his destiny. At the latest, he had to be there next summer. He would have finished his medical training by then and he could be a good doctor to the village.

Next, what to do about Lucy? He could have ten happy months…no, ten ecstatic months—with her and then either leave her or take her to Montreval. And the more he thought about it, the more he became certain that he could not take her.

He thought of his one previous attempt to take a girlfriend to his home—Genevieve. That had been an absolute disaster. Lucy, of course, was different to Genevieve—but not too different. He had thought Genevieve was strong, she had said she was strong. And in the wintertime she lasted less than three weeks. No, Lucy would not fit in at Montreval.

So, do what she had agreed, carry on seeing each other, wait and see how things turned out? Then go to Montreval? It was so tempting. But that would be unfair to her. The decision was already made. It would make things so much harder for her.

There was no point in putting things off. To do otherwise would be unmanly, cowardly, dishonourable. He would tell her that night.

Doing what was right was not always easy.

Lucy had a good shift. She was sorry not to see Marc there, but a smiling sister told her that there were things he had to sort out. Lucy guessed from the smile that the sister had a good idea how things were between them. The gossip would be all over the hospital soon. No matter. She was happy with it.

And as she worked she thought of the previous night, a faint blush coming to her cheeks. There was tonight, of course. Perhaps she would stay with him again.

It was dark when she came out of the building and she saw him waiting for her under one of the yellow lamps. She trotted over towards him, threw her arms round him and kissed him. Who cared who was looking? This was something she was happy, proud about.

'I missed you,' she said, 'but it's good to see you now.'

He said nothing, seemed a bit stiff.

'What's the matter? Bad news from home? I saw you had a letter.'

'Just the usual letter,' he said. 'Things going wrong in the village.'

'Have you been home to your flat yet? I went to the supermarket, picked up some stuff and cooked you supper, a shepherd's pie. My mother's recipe, not a French dish, but you'll like it.'

She was prattling, she knew, but she didn't care. She was happy.

He didn't reply. And suddenly she was afraid. 'What is it, Marc? Is there something wrong? Bad news from home?'

He took her arm—not her hand—and urged her onwards. 'We have to talk,' he said, 'find somewhere where we will not be disturbed.'

He led her through the grounds, and after a moment

she realised he was taking her towards the nurses' home. 'Aren't we going to your flat?' she asked.

'No.' A single, cold, curt syllable. They paced on in silence.

Suddenly she stopped, faced him. She tried to make her voice strong, but she knew there was a quaver in it. 'Marc! There's something wrong and I want to know what it is. Now!'

He took her hand, led her to where a bench was half hidden by dropping branches. They sat side by side and he let go her hand.

'Well?' she demanded.

'This has to end,' he said. 'We have to part. We're getting too…close.'

'What?' She couldn't keep the incredulity out of her voice. 'Is this some kind of a bad joke?'

'I did tell you when we started our…affair that I was not a free man, that in time I would have to go back to Montreal. And that is what this afternoon was about. I have been deceiving myself and you, I thought we could be happy together.'

'We are happy together! You mean more to me than any other man I've ever met!'

She felt him flinch. 'I feel the same. But we have no future.'

Lucy was just coming round to realising that he meant what he said. 'No future? But we have a past. Now you have slept with me you don't need me any more. One more conquest for the French doctor. How many does that make? Does that mean that I can send you a Christmas card?'

'Lucy!' His voice cracked like a whip. 'You are entitled to hurt me but you are also hurting yourself. You know that is untrue.'

'I can't hurt you, you have no feelings.'

'I assure you that I have.' She could hear the tremor in his voice.

There was a moment's silence and then she said, as calmly as she could, 'Will you, please, tell me what brought on this decision? Couldn't you have told me last night, before I shared your bed?'

'I had a letter from my mother. She is ill. Next summer I shall have to take over the running of Montreval. There is no future for you there so we must stop our relationship now to avoid further pain on both sides.'

'You decided I was not fit to go to this place Montreval? You didn't think I should be consulted? I'm a grown woman, I can make up my own mind.'

'In this you must be guided by me. I know you're tough, you would not like to admit defeat. But in time you would be defeated. And I could not bear to watch you getting more and more unhappy. And you would.'

Her voice was quiet. 'I see. So this is the end of our love affair?'

'It must be. But I hope we can remain friends.'

'You must be joking. Goodnight, Marc. Don't you dare try to walk me to the nurses' home, I can find my own way. I'll see you around on the wards. But from now on, only talk to me if it's business.'

She walked the last couple of hundred yards. Pride kept her face straight, she even managed to smile at the nurses coming out of the front door. Only when she was in her room did she fall on the bed and weep.

*   *   *

The following day Lucy found she was being transferred to the delivery suite, and working nights. It
wasn't ideal, but babies chose their own time to be
born. And there was always something comforting
about night-time in a hospital. She found relief in
work, being busy was good for her. And she liked this
best of all, helping mothers through delivery.

A week passed and she hadn't spoken to Marc
again. Sometimes it happened that way.

When she went on duty, she took over from another
midwife. In some ways she thought that was rather
sad—a mother might have to deal with up to a dozen
midwives as she progressed through antenatal care,
into delivery and then to the clinic afterwards. She
thought the old-fashioned way, in which one midwife
stayed with a mother all the way through pregnancy,
delivery and afterwards, might have been more satisfying for mother and child. But efficiency was all-
important now.

She was relieving her friend Maria Wyatt. Maria
pretended to wipe her brow as she came out of the
room, preparing for handover.

'Got a good one for you,' she said. 'Annie McCann,
primigravida, first stage. No need for Syntocinon to
move things along. In fact, no real problems. She's
excited but frightened. Been to all the antenatal
classes, done everything possible. Any good advice
going, she's taken it. Husband is with her. It ought to
be easy.'

'So what's the problem?'

'She's a worrier. Over the past six months she's had
every midwifery textbook possible out of the library.
And she's bought more than a few. Now she and her

husband are experts on everything that could possibly go wrong. Even told me a couple of things that I didn't know. The husband asked me if I was capable of dealing with amniotic fluid embolism. I told him I expected never to come across a case in my entire midwifery career. But if it happened, I'd sent for help.'

Lucy grinned. 'We'll have lots of interesting conversations, then,' she said. 'I might learn something myself.'

But after a couple of hours she wasn't so sure. Annie wasn't too bad, her husband was much worse. Wilfred was a primary school teacher, he had studied childbirth—out of books—and taken copious notes. He had a large notebook. Every time his wife had a contraction or Lucy did a test, he carefully noted it down. Then he asked a question or two. Usually a completely pointless one. 'Is that normal at this stage, Midwife? Is it not a little premature?'

'Quite normal. These things can vary quite a lot, you know.'

Lucy, of course, was filling in the partogram, the step-by-step account of the birth, with every observation carefully recorded. She was a bit surprised to discover that Wilfred had copied out his own partogram. He asked for the results of the observations. Then he would solemnly enter them up in his notebook, smile down at his wife and say, 'All going to our plan so far, dear.'

Lucy felt like telling him that he hadn't done any planning, it was all down to Mother Nature. And Mother Nature had a way of disorganising plans. But she didn't say anything.

Things were going well, it looked like being a

straightforward birth. There was a knock at the door. Lucy checked that Annie was in a suitable state to receive visitors, and shouted, 'Come in.' She turned, her heart lurched. It was Marc.

'May I come in?' he asked. In the delivery room the midwife was boss, until she asked for help. Doctors had to acknowledge her primacy. But, still, some didn't ask. Marc was courteous.

'Of course,' she said, her voice trembling slightly.

'I'm the SHO on duty. I just thought I'd introduce myself. I don't wish to interfere.'

'You're not. This is Annie McCann and she's now into the second stage. Cervix is fully dilated. And this is Wilfred, her husband. Annie, Wilfred, this is Dr Duvallier.'

Wilfred's eyes lit up. He grabbed Marc's hand and said, 'I'm pleased to meet you, Doctor. I've just got a couple of queries about—'

Gently Marc disengaged his hand and said, 'In a moment, Mr McCann. I'd like to take a look at your wife first, if I may. Annie, how are you feeling?'

'Well, I wonder if I might not be ready to stop pushing and start panting,' gasped Annie. 'Sometimes I wonder if I'm not pushing too hard. We must have a vertex presentation with the bead flexed and the occiput anterior.'

Marc turned to Lucy, raised his eyebrows. Carefully, Lucy said, 'Annie and Wilfred are very interested in the birth process. They have studied it at great length. Prepared themselves, if you like. But everything seems to be going fine.' She handed him the partogram.

'I see,' said Marc, and nodded understandingly. He

turned to Annie and said, 'No, you're not pushing too hard. Just follow the midwife's instructions.'

'In general everything seems to be going to…seems to be all right,' Lucy went on. She hadn't wanted to say 'going to plan'.

'Good.' Marc turned and smiled at the patient. 'Annie, you have nothing whatsoever to worry about. Everything seems to be fine. This should be a perfectly normal birth and soon you will have your baby.'

'Every midwife should hope for the best but be prepared for the worst,' Wilfred declaimed, obviously quoting from some textbook.

'And we are prepared,' Marc said. 'I'm on call, there's a team of experts always ready behind me. It's most unlikely that anything will go wrong, but if it does we'll cope. And I'll drop in every half-hour or so. If that's all right, Lucy?'

'Of course,' she said. But, in fact, it wasn't all right. She didn't want to see him, even though she knew that Wilfred would be soothed a little by his presence.

Marc turned to go. 'Do you have a minute, Lucy?' he asked. She followed him out of the room.

'They are OK aren't they?' he asked.

She sighed. 'They're sweet really, just a bit of a pain. Don't worry, I can cope.'

'I know that. I've not seen you for over a week. How have you been?'

'There's no reason why you should have seen me. As to how I've been, well, I've been coping because I have to.'

He sighed. Lucy, please, understand that I did what I did because I thought it for the best—'

She interrupted him. 'Marc, let's get one thing

straight right now. You said everything that was necessary. I understand your position. I don't agree with it but that doesn't matter. I just don't want you to say anything more.'

'So can we be friends?'

She looked at him disbelievingly. 'Friends! No, Marc, we can't be friends. We were lovers. That had to stop. But we can never become just friends. Colleagues certainly, and I will work with you as best I can when I have to. But I would prefer not to work with you, and if you can arrange to keep away, that would be best for me.'

He was silent for a moment and then said in a neutral voice, 'That is very clear. As far as I can, I will respect your wishes.' He turned and went. For a moment she wondered if she had been hard on him. Then she decided she had not been as hard on him as she had been on herself.

She felt inside her collar, gently tugged at the medallion on her gold chain. Love conquers all. What rubbish!

But later she was glad of his professional presence. He had come in once or twice, smiled perfunctorily at her and reassured Annie and Wilfred that all was going well. The birth was progressing perfectly normally but then—she might have guessed—Wilfred started to panic towards the end.

As usual Lucy rang through for another midwife when the birth was imminent. And casually she added, 'Ask the SHO to come in if he can. Nothing serious, but he might be able to help.'

When Marc came in, in spite of being asked twice to move back, Wilfred was leaning over Lucy's shoulder, pointing and saying in a terrified voice, 'It seems to be stretching too much to me, Lucy. Perhaps she should have an episiotomy. Annie, it's all right. I'm here for you.'

Marc took in the situation at once. Taking Wilfred firmly by the hand, he drew him back towards the head of the table. He said, 'Wilfred, we'd like you to hold your wife's hand. That's the best you can do for her now. All is going very well.'

'But I thought that an episiotomy—'

'The midwife and I agree that there's no need for one. If you wish, I'll stay here for the birth. But your job is to comfort your wife.'

'Wilfred, it's coming, it's coming,' screamed Annie, 'Wilfred, I can feel our baby coming.'

'And it's a lovely little boy,' Lucy said.

Wilfred swayed. Lucy saw Marc put out a steadying arm. Then Wilfred fainted and Marc laid him gently on the floor.

'I knew everything would be all right,' Annie said as she nursed her child a little later.

After helping resuscitate Wilfred, Marc left. And Lucy didn't see him again for the next week.

CHAPTER SEVEN

SHE had just come off nights and was trying to get her body clock in order. She was trying to sleep but it was difficult. However, she had to do it. It was always that way when you came off nights.

Lucy had three days off and wasn't sure how she would spend them. For once she didn't have any hopes, any plans. Life seemed to be grey. It was two in the morning and she was thrashing around in bed, tempted to get up, turn on the light and read. But she knew that was not a good idea. She had to sleep. But she was missing Marc. There was a void in her life.

The phone rang. She jerked upright in bed. Who could it be, what could it be? At this time of night it could only be bad news or a mistake or a prank. She picked up the phone. It was none of the things she had feared. It was Marc.

She blinked, tried to make sense of things. His voice was urgent. 'Lucy? I need help, I know you said it was not possible, but just for a while I need a friend and I have no one else to turn to.'

'You need help from me? In the middle of the night?' She was so surprised that she didn't even get angry. 'What sort of help?'

'Do you remember me telling you about my cousin Simone? The one who caused all the trouble? Well, two nights ago she moved from Manchester into a flat here in the city. I've just had a phone call from her.

She is now thirty-six weeks pregnant. She needs to see me and she thinks she might have done something stupid. Like take too many pills. But she's not sure. She wants me to go round and I would like to go round with…a friend.'

Lucy collected her scrambled thoughts. 'You say she might have taken too many pills? Suicide or accident? Marc, send for an ambulance for her. She needs proper care.'

'I can't do that. It'll make things worse. She's hysterical.'

'Better hysterical than dead,' said Lucy.

'True. But she would probably send the ambulance away. I gather that in the past few weeks she has already sent two midwives away before they could complete their examinations.' He paused. 'I must do what I can for her, even though I know she might be just playing tricks again.'

'Why me anyway?' asked Lucy.

'I have seen you working, you are good at settling patients. With me Simone is always a bit combative. But no matter. It was a foolish idea. I am so sorry to have disturbed you. It won't happen again.'

Lucy sighed. 'I won't sleep now anyway. If you want me to, I'll come with you. Will you pick me up outside in ten minutes?'

There was a pause so long that she thought he had rung off. But then he said, 'I'll be there.' Then he rang off.

She rinsed her face, cleaned her teeth, pulled on casual clothes, with a cap over her hair. She thought for a minute and then grabbed the midwife's bag she kept in her room. She was going out in the district soon and she needed to have it ready. Then she went downstairs.

Marc was outside, standing by the big black car. She shivered in the night air and then climbed straight into the car. She said, 'One quick word. It's the middle of the night, we are midwife and doctor, going to see a patient. We have no personal feelings.'

'That might be the best thing.'

She threw her bag onto the back seat and said, 'I'm going to recline this seat and sleep. Wake me when we get there.'

'As you wish.' The car purred quietly forward. She knew the journey would not be long but she didn't want to have to talk to him. Or endure a silence.

She tried but she couldn't sleep. She remembered the last time she had been in this car and what had happened that night. And there was a smell to the seat, a leather, a masculine smell—it reminded her so much of him. But she lay there, eyes closed, breathing heavily.

After a while he said quietly, 'If you're asleep, you'd better wake up. We'll be there in five minutes.'

'I'm ready. I don't want to pry into your family affairs but I need to know more about the patient, Marc.'

'Of course. Simone is my cousin. The daughter of my mother's younger sister, I've known her since she was a baby. She is an only child, a rebel, a trouble-maker. But I'm fond of her—though she can be intensely irritating. She has been spoilt all her life and now I just can't get out of the habit of spoiling her. She has a positive genius for manipulating me.'

'And the baby's father?' Lucy asked with a shiver.

'Don't ask,' said Marc. 'He's just disappeared.'

The car stopped, she sat upright, reached round for her bag. Both stepped out, they were outside a block of expensive flats. 'Not an impoverished student, then?'

He smiled a thin smile. 'Not an impoverished family. And, unfortunately, Simone has her own trust fund.'

He pressed a bell and after a while spoke into an intercom. 'Simone, this is Marc. Let me in.'

'Why don't you speak French to her?' Lucy asked.

'Her English is now as good as mine. And she speaks it regularly to irritate her family. But it works for us because I think it important that you now hear and understand everything that is said.'

They walked upstairs, along a thickly carpeted corridor to where a door was already open. They walked into a dimly lit room. Lucy felt by the door, found a switch and turned on the overhead lights.

'Too much light!' a voice wailed.

'We need to see what we are doing,' Lucy said briskly. 'I'm Lucy Stephens, and for the next few minutes I'm your midwife.' She walked over to the windows, let down the blinds. Then she looked around the room.

It was a large room, expensively furnished but now a complete mess. There were clothes, sheets of music, newspapers everywhere. On most surfaces there were cups and saucers, glasses. In the centre of the room was a big leather couch with pillows and sheets in disorder on it. And in the centre of them, as if in a cocoon, there was a tiny creature with long blonde hair and great blue eyes. 'Are you going to get mad at me, too?' asked Simone. 'Marc is always getting mad at me.'

'I'm a midwife,' Lucy said again. 'I'm not allowed to get mad at patients. I think I'd better examine you.'

'I didn't ask for you. I wanted Marc!'

'Well, you got me. And by the look of this rubbish on the table, you need me.' She pointed to a coffee-table where there was a half-empty wine bottle and a smeared glass, a plate which apparently had once held nuts, a couple of opened bottles of pills.

Marc said, 'Lucy, I thought that perhaps—'

'Why don't you go in the kitchen and make us all a cup of tea?' said Lucy. It was an order, not a request. 'Stay there and I'll call you when I want you.'

Simone glared at her. 'You're a bully, do you know that!'

'I told you, I'm a midwife, trying to do her best for you and your baby. Now, what pills did you take? And when and how many? And how much wine did you drink? Come on, we have to know these things.'

Lucy had come across mums-to-be like Simone before. There came a stage when gentle coaxing and sympathy just didn't work. Then you let the patient know who was in charge.

Simone was shocked, obviously not used to being spoken to like this. 'I didn't drink a lot of wine. Half a bottle or something, I just couldn't sleep. Lucy, you don't know what my life is like! I'm miserable all the time, and I've got this great belly so I can't get into my clothes and I can't go out and I can't sleep and..'

'It's a hard life,' said Lucy.

She picked up the two medicine bottles and looked at the pills. They were mild analgesics and iron tablets.

Not a lot appeared to have been taken, there were plenty left. 'I asked you how many of these you took.'

Simone looked sullen. 'I don't know. I took a couple and I wasn't very happy so perhaps I took some more.'

'You're sure you didn't take anything else?'

'Yes, I'm sure. Think I'm a fool? I should know what I'm taking.'

'So you should. Well, even a full bottle wouldn't hurt you too much. So this time we won't get you to a hospital to have your stomach pumped out.'

That was a vain threat but Lucy hoped that Simone wouldn't know it. Simone looked appalled. 'I didn't take anything else!'

'All right, then. Well, let's have a look at you. Where are your records kept? 'The idea these days was that pregnant women should keep their own notes. It was meant to make them feel that they were in charge of their own future and that of their baby. Lucy didn't think that was a good idea in Simone's case.

Ideally, Lucy should have spent some time talking to Simone, getting to know her, establishing a relationship. But this was the middle of the night and could be an emergency.

The simplest tests first—pulse, blood pressure. Both within acceptable parameters. Then a quick check for oedema—some swelling in the ankles, none in fingers or face. Good.

'I need a midflow urine sample, Simone. Go into the bathroom and get me one.'

With a great sigh Simone flounced out, returned and silently handed Lucy the required sample. Lucy checked for protein, glucose and ketones. All readings acceptable.

'Now, roll over on your back, pull your nightie up and try to lie flat.'

Simone did so. Gently, carefully Lucy ran her fingers over the distended abdomen. She was trying to determine the lie, presentation and position of the foetus, and the engagement of the head. Then she used her Pinard stethoscope to listen to the baby's heartbeat.

She noticed that now she had an audience that was not willing to give way to her, Simone was a lot less distressed than she had indicated to Marc.

Marc should have known that Simone was acting. He wasn't always the ruthless master of his emotions. He was capable of being fooled—and even of knowing it. He was human after all.

Lucy wrote down all her findings and then checked them against the entries made by the previous midwives.

'Things seem fine so far. Now, just lie on your back and pull your legs up.'

Everything seemed fine. But then Lucy wondered. She palpated Simone's abdomen again and then said, 'OK. Pull your nightie down and cover yourself up. I'm going to have a word with your cousin.'

She went into the kitchen and shut the door.

'Well?' Marc asked.

'False alarm. No need to worry about the pills. They were just iron tablets and a couple of mild analgesics, and she's hardly taken any. She was just bored, and since she couldn't sleep decided to wind you up. But there is something. You know she's been playing up with the midwives?'

'I guess so. Why?'

Lucy didn't like letting down her own profession. But… 'I think they might have missed something. I think it's possible that she's suffering from unstable lie and she should go into hospital. If I'm right, she's in danger of cord prolapse. She needs ultrasonography and to be seen by an obs consultant.'

'But are you certain?'

'Not at all. I'm just being careful. But if I was on the district and found a case like this, I'd get her to the obs consultant urgently. I'm a new midwife, you're a training doctor, we just don't know enough. I do know the chances are dozens to one that it will be a false alarm. But if she stays here there's the remote chance that she might lose the baby.'

He thought for a moment and then said, 'I will take your advice. Simone must go to hospital—though the last thing I want is to have her in my department. I'll phone and get her admitted to the Castle Hospital—it's the nearest anyway. I'll talk to whoever senior is on duty.' He looked gloomy, 'I suppose I'd better tell her.'

'I'll tell her if you like, it might come better from me. You just arrange the ambulance.'

Lucy went back into the living room and said, 'Simone, it's probably nothing but Marc and I think that it's better that you go to hospital to be checked up.'

'But I feel fine, now' she complained.

'Marc's phoning for an ambulance,' Lucy reiterated. 'Come with me to your bedroom, I'll help you dress and then you can pack a small case so we'll be ready when it arrives.'

'But I'm not ready! I want to sleep and—'

'Dress and case! Otherwise you'll have to get into the ambulance like that! I'll tell Marc what we're doing.'

Now the decision had been taken, Simone was surprisingly co-operative. She dressed quickly, picked the things she would need. Then Marc came into the room. 'I suppose you've agreed to all this,' Simone grumbled to him. 'It's the last time I phone you for help.'

Lucy had to turn away and smile when she saw the look of incredulity on his face. But all he said was, 'I'm sure it's all for the best.'

'You're both going to stay with me, aren't you?' Simone demanded. 'I can't do this on my own.'

'Only you can have the baby,' Lucy pointed out.

Marc said, 'We can't presume on Lucy any longer, Simone. I will stay with you until you are settled. But it is the middle of the night. Lucy must go home. Lucy, you must take my car.'

Lucy shook her head. 'You'll need it and I can always—'

'Please! It will make me feel considerably better. I have presumed on your goodwill far too much already.' He offered her the car keys.

He had presumed on her goodwill? That was one way of putting it, she thought. What else had he done to her?

'All right,' she said, taking the keys. 'If you trust me with it.'

He winced.

She left his car outside his flat and pushed the keys

through the letterbox. There was light just showing in the sky when she got back to her own room. But she slept at once.

It was almost a joke the next evening. She was in her room, washing her hair, when there was a knock on the door. Lucy thought it must be one of her friends from down the corridor. With her dressing-gown half-open and a towel round her head, she opened the door. It was Marc. And what made it worse was that two of her friends were walking down the corridor behind him. Both grinned broadly. One raised her eyebrows and winked at Lucy. And so Lucy was in an instant bad temper.

'I wasn't expecting you!' she said.

'I am sorry. This is obviously a bad time. May I call back later? I felt I had to speak to you.'

'Come in if you must,' she said rather flustered. 'But you can't stay long. I'm going out to see my parents.'

'Of course.' He stepped into her room and she saw that he held a bunch of flowers. He seemed uncomfortable.

'These are for you,' he said, handing them to her, 'and they come with my deepest thanks. I now realise what an imposition it was, calling on you in the middle of the night. But Simone has that effect on me.'

'These are very nice. I'll put them in water at once.'

'Another thing. One should never try to practise medicine on a family member. You were right and I was wrong. Simone does have an unstable lie She must stay in hospital until the child is born. We—the family—owe you. And we don't know how to repay you.'

'I'm a midwife, there is nothing to repay.'

'Well, then, you are entitled to know a little about Simone. That is, if you wish to know.'

She did want to know. 'Tell me,' she said. 'You can sit on the bed while I dry my hair.'

So he sat. Then he said, 'Simone came to England to study music. It may be that she is talented, but she has never worked hard enough to develop her talent. She had a big argument with her parents, refuses to have anything to do with them. She has her own trust fund and is not reliant on them for money.'

Now he looked angry, Lucy thought. He went on, 'Then a typical story. She got pregnant, said nothing to her family for six months. Then she announced that she didn't love her boyfriend anyway, she had no intention of coming home and could manage her own life. Her father wrote to me as I was the nearest family member and, since Simone had always been fond of me, asked if I could I help in any way. Of course, I said yes.'

'And you've had nothing but trouble since?'

'Nothing but trouble. But she's family. Wouldn't you do what you could for your family?'

'Yes,' said Lucy.

Marc walked out of the nurses' home, managing to do nothing but smile politely at the couple of nurses he met in the corridor. But he was aware of their knowing glances, and wondered what Lucy might have told them. Then he relaxed—just a little. He knew Lucy would have told them nothing.

He needed to be alone. He climbed into his car, drove through the city outskirts and eventually found himself on parkland, overlooking the river. He got out of the car, walked down some steps and sat watching the turbulent water racing past. There was a giant oil tanker in the channel, slowly making its way upstream. A couple of yachts tacked nearer shore. And on the far bank he could see the silver pipes and chimneys of the oil refinery.

He often came here to think. This was where Lucy had first brought him. He gazed down at the black water, stared at the sparking lights across the river. Nothing helped.

He had thought he was in love with her. It had started, as so many affairs did, just as a quick mutual attraction. But that attraction had developed so quickly, it had seemed to have a life of its own. Neither of them had fully realised it. Then he had stopped it—brutally.

No way could he take Lucy home to Montreval. He loved the place, wanted to work there. But no way would Lucy be happy there and no way could he bear to see her miserable. Perhaps in time he would meet some French girl who would love to be the Comtesse de Montreval. But he doubted she would make him as happy as Lucy could. He shrugged. He knew what he had to do.

Of course, Lucy had to meet Marc sometimes. They worked in the same department. She was still in the delivery suite and, as SHO, he was moved from section to section as he was needed. But he still spent a fair amount of time working near her. Mostly it was paperwork, checks of various kinds, and he was on hand if she needed a doctor. So she did come in contact with him. But when they passed in the corridor it would only be a cursory smile or a 'good morning'. And if she saw him drinking coffee or talking in a group, she would keep out of the room.

'What's between you and Marc Duvallier?' Maria demanded.

'There's nothing between us.'

'That's what I mean. All this trouble to be polite, it makes it obvious that there has been something between you—or there's going to be. You're not like it with the other doctors—you're much ruder, and they like it. What has Marc done that you have to be so polite to him?'

'Nothing,' said Lucy. It seemed hard that her evasion wasn't fooling anybody.

When they had to work together she saw that he was a really good doctor. Perhaps because he was slightly older, he had a better understanding of the patients than the other SHOs. They were all good at medicine—Dr Bennet wouldn't have had them otherwise—but Marc was good with people too.

And then came a case they both had an interest in. Astrid Duplessis came in to have her baby. Marc had been the one to keep in touch. He had told Lucy that Kevin was delighted and frightened at the prospect of being a father, that Astrid was happy living with Kevin's parents, and that they had been in touch with Astrid's family. Some kind of a reconciliation was possible. 'I told you that love would conquer all,' he said to her with a sad smile.

'And I didn't believe you. Well, I'm glad to be proved wrong.'

Astrid was pleased to see her, and so was Kevin.

'I'm going to be present at the birth,' he told her. 'Though I'm a bit nervous.'

'There's usually nothing to worry about,' Lucy said. 'Now, stand up there and hold Astrid's hand.'

It should be a straightforward delivery. The cervix was now effaced and dilating, no problems so far.

Lucy checked the outgoing midwife's comments on the partogram. Everything seemed to be fine. Well, she would be kept busy, there would be no time to brood over other things.

'Dr Duvallier will be in shortly,' she told the couple. 'He's got a special interest in this baby. And so have I.'

'We wouldn't have been together if it wasn't for you two,' Kevin told her. 'If it's a boy, we're going to call it Marc.'

'That'll be lovely. Now, I'd just like to listen to the baby's heartbeat.' Lucy took her Pinard foetal stethoscope and applied it to Astrid's abdomen, listened for a minute. 'Good and strong,' she said, and filled in the result on the partogram.

A couple of hours later there was a knock on the door. It was Marc. They smiled at each other in their usual way, polite but blank. 'Just checking my friends,' he said. 'I take it there are no problems?'

'None at all. We won't need a doctor but stay and chat with them for a while.'

She had never been more wrong about needing a doctor.

Things started to go wrong about an hour later. The delivery suite was rather busy so there wasn't another midwife to assist at the birth. No problem. Marc could do it, standing by to take the baby and help if necessary. But she was in charge.

Astrid pushed. There was the head—rather a large one, Lucy noted. But she said encouragingly, 'Nearly there, Astrid! We have the head!'

Then she frowned and glanced up at Marc. He had noticed it, too. The baby's chin was tight against the perineum—in fact, when Astrid stopped pushing, the head seemed to retract a little. Marc raised his eyebrows questioningly, nodded towards the telephone. Was this an emergency? She was in charge, it was her decision to make.

This was not the time to worry the mother. Trying to keep her voice level, Lucy said, 'See if there's anyone handy to drop in. Possibly a shoulder dystocia.' Marc moved swiftly to the phone, but kept his voice down. Astrid had enough to worry about.

Encouragingly, Lucy said, 'We need to get you into another position. Slide down the bed, Astrid, and pull your knees up and out.' The lithotomy position. It gave the midwife the best access for an examination.

Quickly, Lucy administered a local anaesthetic, then cut a generous episiostomy, taking great care not to injure the baby's neck. Then did a vaginal examination. No doubt now. This was a shoulder dystocia. The head could be—had been—born. But the shoulders were too broad to come through.

She knew that shoulder dystocia was rare—perhaps one in every five hundred births. She had only ever seen one, and that had been when she had been a second-year student and had been able to do nothing but watch. Now she was in charge.

Marc returned, murmured that the senior registrar

had been bleeped and was on his way. But they couldn't just wait.

'I'm going to ease the head down towards the floor,' Lucy told him. 'I'd like you to apply pressure to the anterior shoulder and the fundus.'

They worked together. A different angle and perhaps the shoulder would slip through. It didn't.

'Try to rotate the baby?' Marc suggested quietly. 'Bring the posterior shoulder into an anterior position?'

That was the next thing to try. And that didn't work either.

Where was the registrar? Lucy wondered. She needed help! But she kept her face smiling and her voice calm.

'Just a small problem Astrid,' she said. 'Baby doesn't want to come into the world yet, we're having to persuade him.' She had forgotten that Astrid's English was very basic.

Now Astrid was realising that something was wrong and she started to panic. There was a great outburst of French. Lucy didn't understand a word but the feelings expressed were obvious.

Of course, Marc understood. He moved to the top of the bed, stood by Kevin and took one of her hands in his. And he spoke, liquid musical French. Even Lucy felt comforted by the sound.

It was the voice that did it, Lucy knew. Even at that tense moment she knew that the voice had calmed Astrid, had made her believe that all could be well. A great asset for a doctor.

Time was passing. Only one thing left to do.

Lucy eased her hand in behind the baby and felt for

the posterior arm. She was able to push the elbow backwards, then feel for the forearm. She needed to draw it across the baby's chest. At that moment Mike Donovan came into the room, quickly followed by the delivery suite supervisor.

'I can feel the elbow!' she said to Mike. 'Would you like to…?'

Mike came over, ran his fingers over Astrid's abdomen. 'Just carry on, Lucy, you're doing fine,' he said. Then he moved to where Marc had clapped his arm round the terrified Kevin's shoulders and smiled at Astrid. 'All will be well,' he said.

And at that moment, Lucy eased the forearm into place. 'We can carry on now,' she said to Marc. 'Will you come and apply traction to the baby's head? Upwards this time?'

She looked at Mike. Now he was in charge. He could tell her to stand back, but he just nodded and said, 'I'll hang around here a bit longer, if you don't mind. Things seem straightforward now.'

Minutes later, the baby was delivered. A fine healthy baby boy, a delighted Astrid and Kevin. Altogether, a good result.

An hour later they drank coffee in the nurses' room. It was impossible to be reserved with each other after an emergency like that. They had worked together as a tight team, had anticipated each other's wishes. They had been successful, perhaps saved a baby's life. It was a good feeling and it bonded them. Perhaps only for a short time, but while it lasted, it was good.

'We work well together,' she said.

'We've always been good together.'

Then he stood and she saw him, almost deliberately, assume the same blank face with which he had greeted her recently. They were back to the distant relationship they had had before—the relationship that he had carefully dictated.

'I'd better go and write up my notes,' he said. 'Sometimes I do more writing than medicine.' And he left.

Lucy went to the cloakroom, washed her face. She could feel the tears coming. For a while then they had been back to the way they had been before they had parted. And it had been so good.

Marc phoned her in the early evening about three days later. 'I thought you'd like to know. Late last night Simone went into labour early and eventually had to have a Ceasarean. But she's produced a little girl and mother and child are doing well. She's going to call her Lucille.'

'That's a nice name,' said Lucy.

'There have been frantic phone calls between her family and here. I'm in the middle, trying to mediate. Simone says that if her parents come to visit her, she'll refuse to see them.'

'Post-partum mothers are always a bit upset,' said Lucy. 'Just give her time.'

'Yes.' He paused, and even though he was on the other end of the telephone line, Lucy thought she knew how he looked. He was harassed, in doubt. But he went on, 'Simone seems to have very much taken to you. She asked if you'd call in to see her. She'd like to talk.'

'I'll drop into see her if you like. I know she's been a trouble to you but I rather took to her.'

'She took to you.'

'Just one thing. I don't want to visit her when you'll be there.'

'That is understandable.' She couldn't read his voice. 'Would you like to visit in the evening of the day after tomorrow?'

They agreed that Lucy would visit, and Marc would stay away.

CHAPTER EIGHT

LUCY had visited Castle Hospital, of course, but never worked there. It seemed odd to go into a postnatal ward as a visitor, carrying flowers and looking anxious. She felt that she should be in uniform, helping these busily hurrying nurses and midwives. She felt out of place.

'I've called to see Simone Romilly,' she said to a passing nurse.

'Are you family?'

'Just a friend. In fact, I'm a midwife who helped her.' The nurse winced, then pointed to the end of the ward. 'Good luck,' she said. 'I'm sure you know you'll need it.'

Lucy hid a grin. Evidently Simone hadn't changed.

But there was one big difference that was at once obvious. Simone was no longer purely self-centred. She now doted on the tiny bundle in its cot by her bed. 'Hi, Lucy! Look at my baby—isn't she just the most gorgeous thing?'

Lucy ran a practised eye over the tiny form. 'She looks pretty good,' she said.

'I'm calling her after you,' Simone said. 'Lucy into Lucille.'

'Why me? Why not your parents? Isn't that the French custom?'

'Because you were there for me, they weren't.'

'I gather they would have liked to be with you,'

Lucy said. 'You'll have to make up some time you know. And Lucille will need grandparents.'

'Hmm. We'll see. I've got plenty of time to think about the future. Let's consider the present.' Large blue eyes regarded Lucy closely. 'Why did Marc pick you to come to see me in the middle of the night?'

Lucy felt uneasy. 'We've worked together. And he knew I was…available.'

'Is that so? Have you known him long?'

'Just a week or two. But I gather that you've known him all your life.'

'Yes. And surprisingly I get on with his mother, Tante Clotilde. Has he invited you to Montreval yet?'

'No,' said Lucy flatly. 'But I've heard him talk about it and I don't want to go.'

'I like it but not many outsiders do. I'm not surprised he didn't invite you after the evil Genevieve.'

'The evil Genevieve?' Lucy asked, trying to conceal her interest.

'She came one Christmas. I thought Marc was quite keen on her. At first she was keen on him. Or perhaps she wanted to be the Comtesse de Montreval, or perhaps she thought there'd be a lot of skiing. There's no skiing. After dark there's nothing. Anyway, Genevieve lasted three weeks then she paid a taxi driver in the village to drive her to the nearest railway station. Didn't say goodbye but left Marc a note saying the place wasn't for her.'

'I see,' said Lucy. A couple of things made sense now. But she was angry that Marc should have judged her as being no better than this Genevieve. Still…who was to say that she was?

'And after Auguste's death Marc was carrying an awful lot of guilt,' Simone went on.

Lucy frowned. She remembered that Auguste was Marc's brother who had died. 'What guilt?' she asked. She didn't want to pry but…yes, she did.

Simone seemed to want to chatter on. Perhaps she was lonely. 'It was the reason he gave up medicine for three years. When Auguste died, Marc felt he had to run the estate for a while.'

Now Simone looked genuinely upset. 'Auguste loved the valley and the estate, every wet inch of it. He was never happier than when he was working on it. He was in charge and he loved it. Marc was to leave and be a doctor. Then, one summer, the two of then were working on a steep hillside with a tractor. Auguste told Marc that he could go into the village, there was a birth that he might be able to help with.'

Lucy saw a tear run down Simone's cheek. 'Then the tractor overturned and Auguste was trapped and crushed. But he didn't die at once. If Marc had been there, he might have been saved.'

Lucy blanched at the horror of this story. 'So that's why Marc feels he has to go back?' she said.

'There's been a Duvallier in the valley for the past five hundred years. Of course he does. Now his mother is running the place, but it's always been agreed that Marc would take over. He has to.'

'I see,' said Lucy.

She had learned a couple of facts she wished she had known before. They would have made Marc's decision more understandable. Though it still was unforgivable. But just a little, she could feel sorry for him. Just a little.

'I'd better go,' she said. 'I'll come back in a couple of nights to see you again.'

'Will you come with Marc?'

'I don't think so,' Lucy said.

A week later Lucy was called to Jenny Donovan's office. 'Have a seat, Lucy,' Jenny said, 'Help yourself to a drink first.'

Lucy poured herself a coffee, then looked curiously at the other person in the room. What was John Bennet doing there?

'You've been a full-time paid midwife for over a year now,' said Jenny. 'How's it going?'

'I'm enjoying it and I'm learning all the time,' said Lucy.

'Getting wide experience?'

Lucy thought of the different jobs she had done in the past few months. 'You could say that,' she agreed.

'We're getting good reports on you,' John said. 'You're an asset to the department. Now how well do you know Simone Romilly?'

'Simone Romilly? Dr Duvallier's cousin? I've just met her once or twice.'

'Once under rather intriguing circumstances, I gather,' said John. 'However, you made a considerable impression on the young lady. Which is more than anyone else has.'

Lucy looked at him warily. Where was all this leading? 'What's this to do with me?' she asked.

John steepled his hands. 'Her consultant at the Castle Hospital phoned me—in fact, he's a friend of mine. This is all unofficial, you understand. Simone had a hard birth but has made an excellent recovery.

However, there are now psychological problems. And they are made considerably worse by the fact that there is this ongoing row with her parents. The social workers have been in to see her and have got nowhere. The consultant daren't discharge her. And yet he desperately needs the bed.'

'Simone likes her own way,' Lucy agreed.

'Yes, Miss Romilly is an awkward customer. But she has told the consultant she will move out of the hospital. She will go—not home, but to the home of her aunt, Dr Duvallier's mother. Apparently they get on well. Madame Duvallier is willing to take Simone, to look after her.'

'The problem seems to be solved,' Lucy said. 'How does it concern me?'

Calmly, John said, 'Miss Romilly won't fly. She says it scares her. The only way she will go home is if Marc drives her across France, and you go with them as accompanying midwife.'

Lucy was enraged, but somehow she managed to contain her anger. 'Too bad,' she said. 'Tell Dr Duvallier I'm just not interested. He can find someone else to accompany his cousin.'

She could see that Jenny was at first surprised at her reply. But then she frowned, and nodded as if she understood. So now another person knew her secret!

John remained calm. 'The suggestion has not come from Dr Duvallier,' he said. 'In fact, he knows nothing whatsoever about it. The suggestion came from my colleague at the Castle. He believes this would be in the best interests of Miss Romilly and her child, and it would also free up a bed. I said I'd put it to the two people involved—you and Dr Duvallier. The decision is entirely yours.'

'You haven't asked Dr Duvallier? He knows nothing about this?'

'Nothing,' said John. 'But let's ask him now. He's waiting for me in the next office.' He lifted Jenny's phone, dialled a number and said, 'Would you come through, Marc?' Then he looked at Lucy, his expression placid.

It was obvious that Marc didn't know what was going on. He came in, looked surprised to see Lucy there. Then his face settled into the set expression that she knew so well. 'You wanted to see me?' he said to John.

'Indeed I did. I've been in touch with your cousin's O and G consultant at the Castle Hospital. Your cousin, Simone Romilly, says she will go back to France to stay with your mother. But you and Midwife Stephens here will have to take her. I presume you will travel in your car.'

Lucy saw Marc's face go white with anger. 'It's an imposition to try to drag Midwife Stephens into my family affairs. It's not fair to her. My cousin is a conniving, manipulative wretch.'

'True,' John said amiably. 'They think exactly the same at the Castle. But the medical and psychiatric opinions there are that her condition and that of her baby would improve if she got what she wanted.'

'Impossible,' snapped Marc. 'Midwife Stephens just cannot be asked to be involved.'

Lucy decided that it was time that she made a decision. She didn't like having her fate decided by other people. 'If it is in the best interests of the mother and the baby...I'm not happy but I'm willing to go.'

'You wouldn't be leaving your job,' said Jenny. 'Escorting babies is part of it. And we can arrange with the Castle that they pay for you.'

'Dr Duvallier, now it's up to you,' John said to Marc. 'And may I say that I think it in the best interests of all concerned—especially the baby—if you agree. But it will have to come out of your holiday time.'

There was silence. Now he knows what it's like to be trapped, Lucy thought. Whatever he wants, he daren't go against a statement like that from his consultant.

Finally Marc said, 'That is a very kind offer, Midwife Stephens. I know what it must have cost you. Of course, I accept. When will my cousin and her baby be ready to be moved?'

'Tomorrow,' said John.

Lucy walked across to her room at the end of her shift, wondering what she had done. After their break-up she had tried to avoid Marc, and when they had to speak it was kept short and professional. But each time she saw him it was the same. She felt a great surge of emotion—part anger, part sorrow, part love. How could he have deserted her? Why had she agreed to be close in his company for three or four days?

It was to get her used to the idea of them being apart, she decided. If they worked closely together, they would become nothing but colleagues again, being lovers would be in the past.

It would hurt, but ultimately it would be good for her. But there was one thing she had to remember. Whatever happened, she must never, never, never hope to have him back. That way lay madness.

CHAPTER NINE

THE great black Mercedes headed down the M6. Good thing it was so big, Lucy thought. She wouldn't want to be cramped.

The four of them were surprisingly comfortable. Marc was driving, Simone by his side, seat reclined, apparently asleep. Lucy was equally comfortable in the back seat, with the baby in the carrycot firmly strapped by her side. In the boot were three small suitcases, one each for the adults.

Simone had objected strongly that she could not possibly manage with only one tiny suitcase. But Lucy and Marc had insisted. They needed the room for the pram, the cot, baby clothes and all the other necessities that the baby could need.

'It's surprising how quickly you can organise things when you put your mind to it,' Marc said quietly to her. 'I wouldn't have thought it possible.'

'It's only really a long weekend for me. If you can arrange for me to be taken to Lyon, I can fly back to Manchester and be home again in four or five days.'

'You won't be tired by having to sit in a car for hours on end?'

'I went to Spain by coach once,' she said, 'A non-stop trip of twenty-four hours.'

He winced. 'This trip will be a little more civilised than that.'

She was pleased that she could talk to him in this

casual, offhand way. Perhaps the trip wouldn't be too harrowing for her. And she had forgiven Simone. Simone was just…Simone. She didn't function as other people did.

She leaned forward, looked down at her charge. 'You all right, Simone? Comfortable?'

'I'm asleep,' muttered Simone. 'Leave me alone. I just want to sleep.'

'Simone has a reputation for always sleeping on long journeys,' Marc said dryly. She'll sleep all the way if you let her.'

'Anyone nursing needs all the sleep they can get. We'll be up at three this morning while you're in your bed.'

She had wondered how she would conduct herself so close to Marc. But, of course, she wouldn't be too close. They had a mother and child with them. It was hard to think of two more efficient chaperones.

She said, 'I'd like the chance for Simone to feed the baby and change her in two and a half hours or so. Can you arrange that?'

'No problem. There'll be a motorway stop some-where.'

'I'll take Lucille into the Ladies'. They always have a changing station there.'

'There is in most Men's these days,' he said, which surprised her. But, then, why not?

'When will we cross the Channel?' she asked. She had left all the travel arrangements to him. Her job was solely to look after the mother and child. And so far it had been easy.

'We're booked to go through the Channel Tunnel at nine tonight, although we might get there a little earlier. Once through the Tunnel I've booked us into a hotel that is only ten minutes' drive away. But if you don't mind, we'll live on coffee and sandwiches until we get to the hotel.'

'You should know, I'm a midwife, I eat in hospitals,' she told him. 'That's practically my regular diet. Will you want me to drive at all?'

'No!' He was emphatic. 'Not that I don't trust you. But I think that we all should have our own jobs.'

'As you like,' she said, yawning. 'But now I think I'll join Simone and sleep. I was up late last night.'

She wondered if she'd be able to sleep. But she wriggled and got comfortable and closed her eyes. This was the third time she had slept while Marc had been driving. Always she had felt comfortable, happy to leave it all to him.

Before she managed to doze, she thought that it was odd—she was going to France, with Marc. Once she had wondered whether it would be a trip that they would ever make together. How would she get on with his mother? Well, now she was going to France with him. And she didn't have to get on with his mother. And so far she was coping.

It happened after about half an hour. They passed a heavy lorry or something, the car shook slightly and she opened her eyes. She found that she was staring straight into Marc's eyes—in the rear-view mirror, that was. She wasn't sure of his expression, but it altered at once and he looked away. She was sure that the mirror hadn't been tilted that way before. He had altered it so he could look at her. She wondered why. But his expression had been odd. Half sad, half longing. She went back to sleep, she didn't want to think about it.

It was a surprisingly easy journey. They stopped at three-hour intervals. Simone fed the baby, Lucy checked her and then took her, to change her if necessary. Marc accompanied her, carrying the expensive carrycot and then waiting outside the cloakroom. Then they all had the promised coffee and sandwiches.

But by the end of the day, as they were approaching the tunnel entrance, Lucy had tired of the diet. Simone and Lucille both slept almost solidly. And Marc drove on in stolid silence.

She thought this was good. She didn't want to be forced into any kind of intimacy with him. If he didn't talk, then she wouldn't be reminded of how things had been between them. She could manage.

The drive on the wagon through the tunnel was interesting. Not as much fun as the ferry, but a new experience. And when they got through to France, it was dusk.

Marc drove for the promised ten minutes, apparently knowing exactly where to go. And then he turned into a hotel entrance. Lucy frowned. When he had said they would stay in a hotel, she had expected to stay in one of the large chain of motels that were to be found in every large French town. But this was different. There was a long drive to what had obviously once been a chateau of some kind.

As they drew up outside, a couple of men in uniform walked out to greet them. Marc spoke to them in French—of course. But it gave Lucy a shock to be

reminded that English was not his native language.
And his French voice sounded sexier.

He turned to her. 'You'll be shown to your room
and your things taken up. As we decided, you'll be
sharing with Simone and there's a cot ready for
Lucille. I'll knock in five minutes, you can tell me
then if there's anything you need.'

'I'm going to feed the baby,' said Simone, 'and then
I want to feed me. Marc, order me something light and
a salad. I'll have it in my room. And I want half a
bottle of wine.'

'You can have one glass of wine,' Lucy said cheerfully, 'and that's it. But as much bottled water as you
like.'

'All right, then,' Simone said grumpily. 'This is as
bad as being in hospital.'

Marc turned to her. 'When Simone and the baby are
settled, Lucy,' he said, 'I wonder if you'd like to dine
with me downstairs. We have the baby alarm, Simone
and Lucille will be quite all right without you.'

'Downstairs here? Wearing these jeans and this
shirt? I'd be asked to leave.'

He smiled. 'Well, I think you look most…becom-
ing. But if you wish, we can dine on the terrace.'

Then his face became remote again. 'But, of course,
if you are tired, you may have a meal in your room
with Simone.'

He had given her an out. A choice. She paused a
moment and then said, 'I've been cooped up in the
car all day. I've slept a fair amount, I think I would
like to stretch my legs a little. But I want a bath first.'

'Of course,' Marc said. 'I want one myself.'

There were Lucille and Simone to look after first. But when Lucille was tucked up in her cot, and Simone was in bed with a great collection of fashion magazines, Lucy had a bath in the largest bath she had ever seen, and with the largest collection of free toiletries. Afterwards there were the softest of white towels, the size of a bed sheet. She could get used to this.

And as she luxuriated, she wondered why it was that she had decided to accept Marc's offer of dinner. They weren't friends, couldn't be. After what he had been to her it would be impossible to go back to mere friendship. She supposed she was just curious, she'd never been to a hotel like this. And it would be part of her cure. To prove to herself that she could work with him and not be affected.

And she was desperately hungry. The tray brought up for Simone had been wonderful. Yes, that was it, she just wanted to experience things, it wasn't that she wanted to be with Marc at all. And, anyway, she was getting over him wasn't she?

She had brought just one dress rolled up in her case, a simple cotton dress in a shade of pastel blue. It had straps, there was a short jacket to go over it. Before she had got into the bath she had hung it up to let the creases fall out. 'Nice dress,' Simone said when she came out in it. 'You look good in it.'

Lucy decided not to mention that it had come from a catalogue.

She was getting on well with Simone now—in fact, she quite liked her. She would take no nonsense from her, and Simone accepted that. She knew that Lucy was only thinking of her and the baby.

She brushed her hair, put on a touch of make-up.

Then she went, at the time arranged, to meet Marc in the lobby.

He too must have packed carefully. He was wearing the grey linen suit that he had driven down in, but instead of the black sweater there was a fresh white shirt, bright tie. And his clothes had definitely not come from a catalogue.

He looked at her, she could see the appreciation in his eyes. 'You look lovely,' he said. 'I asked for a table on the terrace, but I feel that we should change to the dining room so I can show you off.'

'The terrace will be fine.'

They were shown to their table, her chair pulled out for her and the candles lit. She put the baby alarm on the table.

'Always the efficient midwife,' he said. 'Nothing must get in the way of your work.'

'Nothing will,' she said. 'I'm always super-careful.'

If he thought there was a message for him there, he didn't acknowledge it. He said, 'I've ordered us a bottle of champagne. I know we both need to keep our heads clear, I think this is the best way.'

'As you wish,' she said. She thought that drinking champagne was an odd way of keeping a clear head, but he seemed to know what he was doing.

'Now, what would you like for dinner?'

She blanched when she saw the menu—in French, of course. Half the dishes she didn't recognise. 'I think I need some help,' she said.

So he helped her. She had an asparagus and shrimp cocktail with an amazing orange dressing, lamb stuffed with chestnuts and vegetables of the season, apple pancakes flamed with brandy.

It was not a heavy meal but she thought it was one of the best she had ever tasted. And at the end, a sure sign that she had enjoyed the meal, she felt considerably happier at being with him.

'You didn't tell me that Simone was close to your mother,' she said as she sipped from her champagne flute.

He pondered. 'Simone's parents live in the heart of a town. They have a large modern flat, traffic pours past outside constantly. Whereas, as I showed you, my mother—and myself in time—live in a country castle. Simone has always been a romantic. She thinks it is like living in a castle in a fairy-tale. And my mother loves having her there, though she will stand for no nonsense.'

'And you're not a romantic?'

'No. I love the castle but I am a realist. It may be a romantic-looking building but I have to pay to have the roof replaced. Simone doesn't think of that. And Simone is still enjoying herself rebelling against her background.'

Lucy had to ask. 'Do you ever feel that you'd like to do that yourself? Rebel against your background?'

Of course, he knew the point of her question. 'Not at all,' he said. 'I know what I am to be and I am happy with it.'

But she thought she saw doubt, if not actual misery in his eyes.

He sipped his champagne and went on, 'Incidentally, I should have told you before. Simone's parents extend to you their deepest thanks.'

The waiter came over, brought them tiny cups of coffee and brandy. When he had gone, Marc said, 'I'm pleased that you felt that you could dine with me this evening, I've enjoyed your company. I feel perhaps we can talk now. And, Lucy, I've missed talking to you. It has all been…even harder than I expected. And I expected it to be hard.'

She knew her voice was shaky as she said, 'I miss a lot about you.'

He nodded, looked bleak. 'The day after tomorrow you will see where I live, perhaps understand a little of why I am the way I am, see why I am dedicated to the valley and its people. I would feel better if I thought that you could understand.'

'We'll see,' she said. Then she stood. 'If you don't mind, I think I'd like to go to bed now.'

He had stood, too. 'Of course. I will escort you to your room. You have my room number—any problem at all, ring me. I will arrange breakfast to be served in your room, just after the baby's early morning feed. Then we will make a good start.'

'Whatever you say,' said Lucy.

She had enjoyed the meal. It was bitter-sweet being with Marc. And it was more sweet—or bitter—realising that he felt just as bad as she did.

In many ways it was an easy trip. Probably Simone and Lucille could have managed without her. The baby was especially good and Simone's mood improved every mile they got nearer the castle. But, then, nothing went wrong. And Lucy knew just how bad things could be when things went wrong with a few-days-old baby.

They drove across France by motorway. Lucy decided that French motorway cafés were nicer than

English ones. The weather got warmer. And then, in the distance, they saw a great line of mountains. They were getting there.

Marc had booked them into another hotel, and they arrived at this one considerably earlier. Simone told them that this time she wanted to eat outside, and eat with the pair of them. Lucy thought that was a good idea. She didn't want to be alone with Marc again. It reminded her too much of what might have been.

Last night she had almost felt that they could be together again. She didn't want that. He had decided that it was impossible, and he was probably right. But she couldn't stop herself loving him. Stupid, wasn't it? she thought.

So the three of them were sitting outside, again on a terrace, but this time one with a view across miles of green fields to the blue mountains in the distance. Beside them in her carrycot was Lucille. Every now and again she would gurgle contentedly.

It was hot, they were sitting under an umbrella to protect them from the sun. Lucy felt that she could take off the little jacket she had worn the previous day. They had another wonderful meal. And then they were content to sit there and watch the sun go down.

She looked across at Marc. This evening he was in trousers and open-necked shirt. He was sitting there casually, leaning back in his chair, laughing at something Simone had just said. Lucy looked at the athlete's body, the wonderful profile, the smile that charmed everyone. And she felt a stab of emotion so strong that she gasped.

There was a linen napkin on her lap. She took it, wound it tightly round her hand and squeezed. Last

night she had thought she had been coming to an ac-
commodation with her feelings. She had even thought
it not fifteen minutes ago. Now she knew she could
do no such thing. She loved him as much as she ever
had. What was she to do now?

She could survive. She would have to survive. But
after this short trip, when she was forced to be with
him, she would make sure that they never met again.
There was always work for a midwife. She would
move from the Dell Owen Hospital. Perhaps she might
move out of the town completely. Just as long as she
didn't have to meet him.

Next morning was different. Lucy woke early, sat in
bed waiting for breakfast to be brought for them. Then
she went to open the shutters to look out. They had
had two days of sun. But now the sun had gone. So
too had the view of the mountains in the distance, they
were shrouded in mist. It was going to be a gloomy
day.

They got off to an early start, drove upwards
steadily. After an hour there were the first splashes of
rain on the windscreen, then a sudden sharp squall.
That settled down to a steady, non-stop drumming on
the roof. 'Typical mountain weather,' said Marc. Then
he peered at the horizon and said, 'And I don't think
it's going to clear.' He seemed quite happy with the
situation.

They were driving out of the well-cultivated land,
too. As they ascended, the villages and towns were
less frequent, they didn't have the air of prosperity that
could be seen lower down. They had turned off the
motorway onto what was supposed to be a main road,

but there wasn't much traffic on it. And soon they turned off that.

Now they were on a small winding road, going upwards all the time. Lucy was glad that they had the four-wheel-drive. And the rain was a hissing, pelting force. They had to drive slowly. And though it was the middle of the day, Marc had to turn on his headlights. Because they were in a narrow valley and the cloud and mist pressed even lower, it seemed like night time.

Finally they turned off into an even narrower valley. 'The entrance to Montreval,' Marc said laconically. 'Fifteen miles of this and the road stops. And there is the village. We won't meet much traffic. Not a lot goes to Montreval—or comes from it.'

Simone was asleep. And Marc appeared to have become more and more content as they neared his home.

Now the rain was booming on the car roof. He drove slowly, carefully. In places Lucy could see the water rushing in sheets across the road. The odd farmhouse they saw looked either impoverished or abandoned altogether. Lucy caught glimpses of rockfaces, of drenched stands of spindly trees.

And then they turned the sharpest corner of all and Marc stopped the car. 'First view of home,' he said. 'There's the castle I was born in. For me that is home. And I don't know whether I love it or hate it.'

Lucy leaned over to peer through the rapidly moving windscreen wipers. Well, yes, she supposed the castle and the surroundings were a bit fairy-tale. But they needed the sun. Now everything looked grey and desolate.

She glanced at Marc, surely there should be some

feeling of gloom brought on by this weather. But there was none. He seemed happy, his face smiling.

'May as well carry on,' he said. 'I hope my mother's got our rooms warmed.'

Simone struggled into consciousness and said, 'She will have. Your mother's a great hostess, Marc. I'm looking forward to staying with her. And she'll dote on little Lucille here.'

'My mother doesn't dote on anything or anyone,' said Marc. 'She is above all practical. And what little Lucille here will do is remind her that it's about time that I produced an heir for the family.'

'The weather must be fine sometimes,' Lucy said weakly.

'Sometimes,' Marc agreed. 'In fact, spring and early summer here are magic. As I told you, you should see the wildflowers. And for that we put up with the rain.'

'Who wouldn't?' Lucy asked.

Simone was staring, apparently quite content, at the rain beating against the window. 'I'm always happy here,' she said. 'It's strange. Marc is happy here but in a different way. I can feel that whenever he comes here he has to work. But Tante Clotilde looks after me. She doesn't push me, like my parents do. And Marc pushes himself, he likes it. Here I can stay and just be.'

'What about your future?'

Simone shrugged. 'I'll stay here for a few weeks— or months even. Tante Clotilde needs a companion and she can help me bring up Lucille. After a while I'll think of taking up my music again. Apparently my parents have arranged for me to be seen from time to time by a consultant in Lyon, he'll keep an eye on me.'

Lucy had to ask. 'What about Lucille's father? Will you be in touch with him?'

The reply was all the more emphatic because it was casual. 'No. I don't need him, or anything he could give me. I'm happier on my own.'

Happier on my own. Seems to be a family trait, Lucy thought, but said nothing.

There was no sign of the hysterical patient Simone had been in England. She was calmer now, this place was good for her. But even after only a few hours Lucy was feeling hemmed in. There was a claustrophobic feel to the village and the valley it was in. Perhaps she could just see why Marc thought that she would not be happy here.

They were in a vast room, with stone walls and floor, but definitely very warm. There was a big double bed for Simone, a cot for the baby. Adjoining was a bathroom, with a large old-fashioned bath perched on four feet and with gleaming brass taps. Plenty of hot water, too.

Lucy had the room next to Simone's. There was a connecting door and if it was left open Simone could call her if she needed help. But there was unlikely to be any need. Simone was happy now.

Lucy went to join Simone at the window. Grey clouds swept over the village below them, there was hardly anyone to be seen. It was nearly autumn, this should be a time of beauty. But all Lucy could feel was depressed.

'We'd better go down for dinner,' Simone said,

'Tante Clotilde likes punctuality. She's arranged for a maid to come and sit with Lucille.'

'Perhaps I could have something on my own up here,' Lucy suggested, 'so you and your family could—'

'No!' There was a show of Simone's old spirit. 'You dine with us! You are a friend, not a servant. And I know Marc would be angry if you weren't there.'

'It's the same dress, then,' Lucy said gloomily. 'If I'd known I'd be having dinner every night, I would have packed three.'

They had arrived at the castle about three hours previously and been greeted by Marc's mother. For once, Lucy had guessed right. Madame Duvallier was everything she had expected.

She had been tall, erect, discreetly made up, with white hair carefully arranged. Her dress had been of grey silk—expensive without being obtrusive. Lucy had thought she could see some of her son's character in her face.

She had greeted Simone and Marc happily but calmly. Both had kissed her on each cheek. There had been considerably more emotion shown over Lucille.

Then, in very good English, Lucy had been made welcome. Her hand had been shaken, she had been thanked for what she had done for Simone and Lucille.

'It was a pleasure, Madame,' Lucy had said. She had asked Marc before hand what she should call his mother. She knew that if Marc had got to know her family, he would have been calling her mother Mum within a couple of weeks. But she didn't think that this would happen here.

A maid had been instructed to take them to their rooms, their bags would be brought up, a drink would be sent. Clotilde had business to discuss with her son, they would meet at dinner later.

Lucy went to get changed out of her jeans and shirt. It was nearly dinnertime and she was not looking forward to it. She wondered how Marc would be. Since they had entered this wet valley she had felt that he seemed more and more distant. He took a pleasure in this place that she couldn't feel. He had smiled but said very little. Well, she would be out of it all tomorrow, and she didn't know whether she was pleased or sorry.

The maid entered the room, went straight to Lucille's cot and smiled down at the child. She was middle-aged, the mother of three children herself. Lucy could tell that she was a more than competent nursemaid.

Simone was now ready. She led Lucy out of the room and the two of them stood at the head of the staircase. 'You know,' said Simone, 'we've been together for three days now and yet, with Lucille being with us, and Marc most of the way, we haven't had the chance to have a proper chat. So how are you getting on with my wonderful cousin?'

'Sorry?' They were in shadow at the moment, Lucy was glad because it would hide her tell-tale flush. 'I like working with him, we get on fine.'

Simone laughed. 'Don't try to fool me. You're in love with each other, aren't you?'

'Certainly not!' Lucy was sure that her pinkness had not gone away.

'Don't forget, I've known him since I was a baby. I've seen the way he looks at you when you think he's not looking. And I've seen the way you look at him. The last couple of nights I've been surprised that you didn't try to sneak out of our room to go to see him.'

'Simone! He's the doctor, I'm the midwife. We're looking after you and Lucille. That's all there is be-tween us.'

'Of course,' said Simone. 'Lucy, I'm very fond of you, but why do you think that I demanded that you and Marc drive me here?'

'To be awkward?' Lucy suggested.

Simone nodded cheerfully. 'Partly that. But I wanted to do something a bit right for once. I wanted to get you and Marc together for a while.'

'You've done that. But now I'm going back.'

'Lucy! Put up a fight for him!'

'I've tried. All I got was hurt.'

They went down the stairs and Simone led her into the dining room. Lucy noticed that Clotilde had changed her dress but that Marc had on the same clothes as before. He must have some clothes stored here. She wondered if he had stayed as he was to make her feel comfortable. She liked him for that.

It was a formal dinner, served carefully. Lucy had the impression that the food was good—but she tasted none of it. There were candles on the table—but this was nothing like the candle-lit meal she had had with Marc two nights before.

Everyone was at pains to make her comfortable. 'We will speak English all evening,' Clotilde had said at the beginning of the meal, and so that was decided.

Lucy had to be included in the conversation. She would have preferred it if they had talked in French, and left her alone.

Clotilde questioned Lucy about her care for Simone and the baby. Truthfully, Lucy was able to say that she had noticed a steady improvement in both as they had crossed France, and an even greater one when they had reached the castle. That gave Clotilde a small smile of pleasure.

'I hope you will be able to stay a little time with us,' she said. 'I would like you to see the castle and the village in sunlight. Though the forecast is bad.'

For various reasons, that was the last thing Lucy wanted. 'Thank you, Madame, but I must get back to work. If I can take a bus or train to Lyon, then I can catch a plane there.'

'I want you to stay longer, Lucy!' said Simone.

'Lucy must get back to work, Simone,' Marc said. 'She was only allowed to leave by the kindness of the hospital management.'

So that is that, Lucy thought. That makes things quite clear.

Halfway through the meal a man came in and whispered something to Clotilde, who smiled at everyone. 'The trouble with living in the country. There has been a mudslide, the road is now blocked.'

Seeing Lucy's look of dismay, Marc said, 'Don't worry, Lucy, we're used to this. The road will be cleared tomorrow, you'll be able to leave by lunchtime the next day.'

'Or you could make it an excuse and stay,' Simone said hopefully.

* * *

Lucy hadn't wanted to stay an extra day. She had breakfast in her bedroom with Simone the next morning, and then there was a knock on the door. It was Marc, dressed in rough clothes, boots on his feet. He held a bag out to her and said, 'I'm playing at being a country doctor. I'm going to make a few calls in the village, see a couple of cases I'm interested in. I thought perhaps you might like to come with me, see the kind of work I intend to do. And you could definitely be a help with some of the babies.'

'What's in the bag?'

He grinned. 'My mother has sorted it out. Not a midwife's uniform, but clothes suitable for wandering around a wet village.'

'I'll be down in ten minutes,' said Lucy. It would be bitter-sweet time spent with him. And she was interested in the work that was calling him here.

Marc explained that a doctor called at the village three times a week and held a surgery in the back of an old shop. 'But Dr Malville is getting old, he should have retired years ago. He keeps on going because he enjoys it and he feels he has to. I phoned him early this morning. He can't get through so he asked me to make a few calls.'

It was medicine of a different, old-fashioned kind. And after the initial shock, Lucy thought that she liked it. First of all, there seemed to be plenty of time. They called at the home of an old man who had an ulcer on his leg. He was pleased to see Marc, he was introduced to Lucy and was equally pleased to see her, and then there was a good ten minutes' general chat before his leg was examined. Then Lucy offered to dress it. A general shaking of hands all round and they walked out into the wet street.

'Different to English medicine?' Marc asked with a grin.

'I don't know. The pair of you were talking so fast that the only word I understood was *bonjour*.'

'You need to live in a place to learn the language. Now, Michelle Malraux is having trouble with her six-month-old baby. Perhaps you can help here.'

A hard tramp through a warren of streets and they arrived at the Malraux house. They could have been quicker, but practically every passer-by recognised Marc, stopped him, shook his hand and had a swift conversation.

'I'm glad this rain is driving people off the streets,' Lucy muttered, 'or we'd never get anywhere.'

'Don't you like it? Isn't it more friendly than an impersonal city?'

She had to agree. 'I suppose it is,' she said.

Michelle's baby wasn't feeding properly and wasn't thriving. Lucy and Marc made a detailed examination, Marc asked questions of the worried mother and translated the answers to Lucy. 'What do you think?' he asked eventually.

She shook her head. 'I just don't know. I suspect it's some kind of allergic reaction. I think we can ease this constant crying for a while but, Marc, this diagnosis is beyond us. This baby needs to be seen by a specialist who has access to a lab and who can order all sorts of tests.'

'I agree. But getting the baby to the nearest hospital will mean a two-day stay away. I'll see what I can organise.'

There were other calls. Twice, Lucy's skills were needed. She advised a young mother about breast-feeding, checked a baby's hips—all was well. And on two more occasions Marc decided that the patient had to be seen at the hospital.

At midday they called in at a café, stood at the counter and had a strong coffee, served in a bowl. 'I feel very French,' she said. 'Where's the man with the accordion?'

'He comes in later. Are you enjoying the day, Lucy?'

'I am. I like this kind of medicine.'

'And do you see why I want to come back and build a clinic here? Get more professionals involved, so there's no need to travel? And don't forget, we're just looking around the village. There are farms and hamlets up in the mountains. For them, just getting to the village can mean two or three hours' travel.'

'I see what you mean,' Lucy said. 'I just wish it didn't rain so much.'

She did enjoy her day, and when they returned to the castle that night she could see why Marc wanted to return to Montreal. For a while she had thought it had been ambition bringing him back, the need to establish a well-known and probably profitable clinic. Now she saw that it was a simple need to serve.

After dinner both Lucy and Simone said they were tired, and went up to see to Lucille together. Marc accompanied them. He took Lucy's arm, held her back for a moment. He said, 'I'll be staying here another four or five days, I arranged it with John Bennet. My mother says there are more things to look over and sign. But tomorrow I will drive you to the nearest station. There will be a chance for us to talk a little.'

'Have we anything to talk about? Just drive me there, Marc.' Then she ran to catch up with Simone.

There was some comfort in doing the tasks she was expert in. The baby was bathed, changed and fed. She liked helping Simone, but there was no doubt she wasn't really needed now. Simone could cope easily. Lucy said goodnight and went to bed.

She was tired but she couldn't sleep. She thought about Marc. Now she had seen him in the place he had described, perhaps she could understand a little. This castle, this village, they hadn't changed much in the past hundred years. Now she could comprehend his love of the place. She liked the kind of medicine he practised here. Marc belonged here, came alive here. And he was right about one thing. This was not the place she would choose to live.

Occasionally he had caught her eye. Perhaps there had been a plea for understanding in it. And perhaps she did understand.

And then she slept. There was no sound but the rattle of rain on the window.

CHAPTER TEN

'Lucy, wake up! Wake up now!' Someone was shaking her shoulder, but she didn't want to wake. However, she had to. She reached out for her bedside light and turned it on. It was three in the morning. And there was Marc, fully dressed, looking down at her.

'Don't make a noise,' he said. 'We don't want to wake Simone.'

She was still befuddled, half-asleep. Marc was in her bedroom. What did he want? Did he want to get into bed with her? She'd like it if he did. But then she came more fully awake.

'Is everything all right? Simone and Lucille OK?' Her obvious first question.

'They're both fine, sleeping soundly. I've just looked in, written Simone a note. They don't need you now anyway.'

'So what is it, then? Don't tell me you want a serious talk at this hour of the morning.' She was feeling irritated, didn't know what was happening.

'No. Someone just called round, there's a problem in the village. We need a midwife. Will you help?'

'Of course I will.' She waved him away. 'I'll get dressed. I've got my bag here. I'll see you downstairs.' She dressed as quickly as possible, this time back in the jeans, shirt and sweater she had worn to cross France.

Marc had been different when he had come into her

164

room. Now they were doctor and midwife again. She liked that.

He was waiting for her downstairs, wearing a heavy oilskin. There was an older man with him who was wet through. 'This is Claude Saulnay, father of the woman in question,' Marc said. 'He brought the message. He knows that I am home and that I am a doctor.'

He offered her an oilskin coat and hat. 'It's raining even harder,' he said. 'I suspect that we are going to get soaked anyway, but we'll do the best we can. I'd send for an ambulance, but it wouldn't get through until morning and a helicopter couldn't land in darkness. So it's up to us.'

The three of them ran out to the Mercedes, the rain, if anything, harder than ever. Claude climbed into the back, and Lucy saw to one side that there was a battered, mud-spattered little French car. It must be Claude's.

They set off into the dark, the headlights illuminating little but the silver rain. They passed a few houses, and then they seemed to be driving straight up the side of the valley. Lucy felt the car skid sideways a couple of times, she didn't like it.

To take her mind off the journey she asked about their patient. 'Helene Dubois, primigravida. Baby apparently coming, about a month prem. Usually Helene lives in the village but when her husband is away during the week she moves in with her father. The trouble is, Claude lives halfway up the mountain.'

'A regular pregnancy so far?'

'Apparently so. In cases like this, when there's any likelihood of an emergency, the mother is moved into the nearest hospital. But this should have been a straightforward birth.'

He had been driving more and more slowly. Lucy felt the car lurch, skid sideways and then stop. Marc cursed in French. Lucy didn't know what the words meant, but guessed they weren't very nice.

The engine screamed, the car seemed to heave itself forward and then stop again. It inched forward. There was a great outburst of French from Claude in the back seat, Marc replied equally rapidly. Then there was silence.

Lucy could tell by the set of Marc's neck that he was worried. 'Come on, tell me,' she said.

'I told you that Claude lives halfway up the mountainside. A little wooden farmhouse, perched on a slope. Well, we don't have avalanches here. We have mudslides. Rain gets under the turf, mixes with the soil and forms a great blob of mud. But the turf holds it back. Then in time it all bursts and you can have a wave of mud five or six feet high sliding down the hillside. Nothing can hold it, it carries everything before it. If a slide hits Claude's farm, it will sweep it down into the valley. I don't like you risking your—'

'We'll have to get this woman out,' said Lucy. 'Load her into the car and carry her down to the castle or somewhere. It's not ideal but it's better than her taking her chance with the mudslide.'

'That's if we can get the car—'

As he spoke the car skidded again, more violently than before, there was a jerk as the wheels on the driver's side dropped into a ditch or something and the car tilted over so far that Lucy thought they were going to roll over. She screamed.

'Open your door, jump out and get away from the car,' Marc snapped. 'Don't argue, just do it.'

She did as he said, and was instantly battered by the rain. She saw Claude jump out of the back door, he came to join her. Then Marc came out of her door. Cautiously he walked round to the far side, presumably to see what they had fallen into.

He was behind the car. And Lucy screamed again as she saw it slide backwards and then slowly, almost with dignity, roll onto its side. Where was Marc?

She ran forward, slipping in the mud. Dimly, through the driving rain, she could see him kneeling by a post, his hands clutched together in front of him. 'Marc, are you all right?'

Claude was now by her side. Marc spoke to him first and Lucy could tell by the rasping of his voice that he was in pain. Claude moved away, and Lucy knelt in the mud next to Marc, her hand on his shoulder. 'What's wrong? Come on, you've got to tell me.'

She was soaked, muddy, tired and scared. All she wanted was to get away, run back to her warm bed. But this was no time for panic, for emotion of any kind. She was a professional who had a job to do.

'When the car slipped backwards it trapped my hand between its side and this metal post. Crushed it a bit.'

'You don't get crushed "a bit". If I could see, I could...'

Suddenly the two of them were illuminated by the brightest of lights. 'I always keep a torch in the back of the car,' Marc told her. 'I sent Claude for it.'

'Let me see your hand.'

He held it out and she took it gently. Hands were

one of the most sensitive parts of the human body and hand injuries were always agonising. And this was a bad injury. Rain spattering on the hand washed the mud and the blood away. The fingers had been squashed, had split so there were long cuts that needed suturing. And she was certain that there were bones broken. As to damaged nerves, there was nothing she could do about those.

'Tell Claude to fetch your bag and mine. Marc, you've got to get to hospital!'

First he spoke to Claude, who handed her the big torch and went to the car. Then he said, 'Well, that's a bit of a problem. There'll be no medical help till morning. And there's a pregnant woman up the road. Now, Claude will lead you down to the village, you'll be all right with him leading. I'll go up to the farm-house and—'

'No. I'm going up to the farmhouse,' she said.

'I will not permit it! I will not let you put your life in danger.'

'You've got no choice,' she said calmly. 'First, I can make up my own mind and I'm going to. I don't need any permission from you. Second, you'll be quite incapable of delivering a baby with that hand. You go with Claude and I'll go and deliver the baby.'

As she spoke Claude came back, holding out their two medical bags. She opened her own bag, pulled out a dressing and wrapped it roughly round Marc's hand. 'That will have to do until I can get a closer look.'

'I don't want you up there,' he said.

'But I'm going. Hard when you can't have your own way, isn't it?'

There was silence for a moment, then another torrent of French to Claude. Claude replied, apparently repeating the instructions he had been given.

'You and I are going up to the farmhouse together,' Marc told her. 'Claude is going to the village, will organise what help he can. But there'll be none till daybreak. The farmhouse is about another half-mile.'

'Let's get started. There's a frightened, lonely girl up there, thinking she'll have to give birth on her own.'

It was a hard climb. They took a bag each. She held the torch because Marc had no spare hand. By now they couldn't have been more wet, but fortunately it was still not too cold.

The mud dragged at them, made them slip, made each step an individual effort. At times she thought she had been staggering upwards for five minutes and had got nowhere. Up one step, slide down two.

She was suffering. What must it be like for Marc, suffering the trauma of a shattered hand? She didn't like to think. 'Are you OK?' she asked.

'Just keep going. I feel fine.'

She had a further twinge of fear. His voice wasn't as strong as it had been. She knew that shock and exertion could kill. He should be lying down, being comforted, not pushing his body to its very limits. Even if he only fainted, what could she do?

But now she could see a light ahead, the farmhouse was in sight. Together they managed the last few feet, waded across to the front door and opened it. They stepped inside. Lucy had been wondering if they would ever make it.

'Allô, Helene! C'est Docteur Duvallier!'

From somewhere there came the sound of more rapid French, this time in a woman's voice. 'No great problems so far,' Marc told her. 'We've got time to get organised.'

The house was neat and clean, not like some places Lucy had visited when she was making home visits. She didn't like dripping rain and mud onto the polished stone floor—but she didn't have much choice. She threw off the now sopping oilskin and followed Marc.

The bedroom was on the ground floor. There was a great bed with an ornately carved high headboard and footboard. A pale-faced young woman was in it, talking to Marc. She looked up and smiled at Lucy. It was obvious that she had been lonely and frightened, panic-stricken even. Now she had help, things were better.

Marc said, 'Helene says she's all right for a minute. Contractions a few minutes apart and now we're here she feels much happier. You're to take off your wet things and throw them into the bath. There are cupboards and drawers through there, you're to help yourself to her clothes. I'll borrow some clothes of Claude's.'

'Stay with her till I come back,' said Lucy.

She rummaged through the cupboard, found some clothes that would do. Then she went into the bathroom, as directed dropped her wet clothes in the bath, towelled herself dry and dressed. There was nothing she could do about her hair—there was no hairbrush to borrow.

She went back into the bedroom, looked at Marc's white face and the sodden dressing on his hand, the bloodstains coming through. 'Can you undress yourself?' she asked.

There was a tiny grin. 'I will manage somehow.'

'It's just that I don't want you fainting and bashing your brains out on this stone floor. Now, go and get changed, keep warm and sit in the kitchen. Don't move till I get there. You're going into shock. I'll look at Helene here and then see to your hand.'

She opened her midwife's bag, and smiled down at Helene. She wondered how she'd cope, not being able to speak the language. As if guessing her thoughts, Marc turned in the door and said mockingly, 'The French for "push" is "*poussez*".'

'I know that! Now, go and do as you're told.'

She examined Helene, took the necessary observations. The baby seemed to be doing fine. Good heartbeat. She had a blank partogram form in her bag, it was second nature to fill in the details just as if she were in the delivery suite at home. She expected that the French would have some equivalent. It seemed as if it was going to be a perfectly straightforward birth, the kind she had supervised often.

Helene was a perfect patient. Now she had help, she seemed quite content to let nature take its course. The fact that she couldn't understand English didn't seem to bother her. And surprisingly Lucy found that they were able to communicate remarkably well.

She patted Helene on the shoulder, pointed that she was going into the kitchen, held up her fingers and pointed to the clock to indicate that she would be five minutes. Then she indicated her hand. Helene nodded. She'd be all right on her own while Lucy saw to Marc's hand.

Lucy went into the kitchen and put the kettle on the gas stove. Then she searched the cupboards and found coffee and sugar. She made Marc a cup, gave it to him. 'I don't take sugar!'

'Today you do. Treatment for shock. Now, I'm going to check your blood pressure and heart rate.' She rested her hand on the side of his face. 'You're getting cold. I'm going to get you a blanket.'

'Lucy, I am not going to let you—'

'Yes, you are! You brought me here, but now I'm here I'm in charge. So let's have a look at that hand.'

She wasn't a nurse but she managed to keep her expression calm as she examined Marc's hand. She took what was necessary from his bag, cleaned the wounds as best she could and then held them together with butterfly stitches. A dressing followed and then she fashioned him a sling. 'Last thing, analgesics,' she said.

His face was white again. In spite of all her care she had had to hurt him. But he said, 'I don't need any painkillers.'

'You do. One thing a midwife learns is how to assess pain.' She looked through his bag. 'I'm going to give you diamorphine. Suffering pain when you don't have to is just foolish.' It only took a minute to give him the injection. 'Now, lie back and try to relax. I'll be next door and if I need you to translate, I'll call you.'

She went back to Helene. Things were progressing normally. Lucy sighed with relief. Yes, this should be a normal birth and she had enough equipment in her bag to make sure that it was a safe one. She let Helene squeeze her hand as another contraction hit her.

Then the lights flickered, went out and came on again. Lucy thought she felt the house tremble. There was an outburst of French from Helene. Lucy just smiled encouragingly and shook her head. What else could she do?

There had been the dual problems of Helene and Marc. She had quite forgotten the biggest problem of all. What about a mudslide?

She went to the kitchen, where Marc was shining the torch out of the window. 'Mudslide,' he said. 'Look, you can see where it washed past. That was just one. The next could be far worse. Lucy, there's no need for you to risk your life. You told me the birth was going to be straightforward. I can manage so why don't you go down the path and I—?'

'Tell you what,' she interrupted, 'I agree. No need to risk life. So you go down the path and I stay here.'

'That's ridiculous!'

'Why is it? It makes sense to me.' She looked at him assessingly. 'Marc, I think you're basically an honest man, so give me an honest answer to this question. Never mind that you want to be macho and look after me at the risk of your own life. What are the chances of us being killed if we stay here?'

The question seemed to hang between them and the silence went on and on. Finally he said, 'I think that anyone who stays in this farmhouse stands a fair chance of being killed if there's another mudslide.'

'Then we ought to live wildly while we can.' She took his head between her hands, kissed him fiercely on the lips. 'We might be killed in a minute so let's live for the minute. I know you've got problems, know you've got duties. But I want you to know, Marc

Duvallier, that I love you. I love you, I said. It's a word that neither of us has used so far. And if I'm killed in the next hour or so, my dying thought will be of you.'

An urgent call came from the next room. 'Lucy, Lucy. Come.'

'Sounds like work is calling,' she said.

When she came back fifteen minutes later, Marc was asleep. Thank goodness for analgesics. And it was a good natural reaction to trauma and pain. She put another blanket over him and left him.

After that, she had work. They felt one more small tremor as they were hit by something, but both she and Helene were busy. Helene had intended to go to hospital, but everything went smoothly and eventually she was holding a newborn son to her breast and crying tears of joy. Lucy was crying, too. She always enjoyed this bit.

Lucy tidied up, tried to make sense of Helene's French. She felt that she'd done a competent job in difficult circumstances. And for some reason she felt in no danger.

She peered out of the window and for the first time saw a clear sky, the odd star, the suggestion of dawn in the distance. All was well. She pulled up a chair to the side of Helene's bed and yawned. Now she was very tired. For just five minutes she could close her eyes.

She was woken up by the loudest noise she had ever heard. She was not the only one. She also heard the tiny wail of a disturbed newborn. The noise got even louder. Now Helene was awake, too, shouting at her in French. Lucy ran into the kitchen.

The noise got impossibly louder then diminished to a clatter. She joined Marc, who was standing by the window. 'Help is at hand,' he remarked. And she saw, not fifty yards away, a helicopter. Men in uniform were running towards the farmhouse. She went outside, waved to them. And as she looked around she saw a great smear of mud had passed within feet of the farmhouse. If it had hit them…

She looked at the village below. There was Claude, toiling up towards them. She waved to him, tried to indicate that it was good news. He waved back. Then she went into the farmhouse again.

The crew from the helicopter were very efficient. Helene and her baby were prepared for a trip to hospital, and a paramedic trained in midwifery was looking with approval at Lucy's partogram. The details were clear in French or English. Then Lucy went to see Marc, who was deep in conversation with another paramedic who was examining his hand. 'You're going to hospital to have your hand seen to properly,' she told him. 'We both know that you need to see a neurologist.'

'But what about you?'

'There's nothing wrong with me. A doctor needs his hands. Get yours seen to.'

'You should come with me to the hospital!'

'No need at all. Claude is coming up, I'm sure he'll get me back to the castle.'

'But we have things to—'

She bent over and kissed him. Quickly, like a friend. 'Forget anything I said last night,' she said. 'I was scared, I didn't know what I was saying. It never happened. Now, you're keeping Helene and her baby waiting. Off you go.'

She felt him watching her as she left the kitchen and started to walk down the path. Perhaps five minutes later there was the deafening roar of rotors again and the helicopter clattered into the air. She didn't look back at it.

Claude spoke no English. He had seen the helicopter, knew it was the medical one and was worried. But Lucy calmed him. She smiled a lot, remembered what she could of schoolgirl French. '*Petit garçon*', she managed—little boy. '*Helene heureuse*'—Helene happy. '*Tous bien*'—all OK.

She pretended she had a baby in her arms, rocked him and smiled. There was a big smile back from Claude—and a loud kiss on each cheek.

Then he helped her down into the village. As they staggered and slipped downwards, Lucy looked at the great slides of mud that had passed so close. If one of those had hit…but it hadn't. They passed the mud-stained Mercedes, forlorn on its side. Lucy looked at it and shivered.

By now she was almost past feeling, this was a greater fatigue than any she had felt in her life before. She got down to the village, someone loaded her into a car and she was driven to the castle. And Clotilde was there to meet her, as calm as ever. Even at that hour she looked smart. Lucy was conscious of her borrowed clothes, of her hair being a mess.

She was surprised when Clotilde took her hands and kissed her gently on both cheeks. 'We, the family and the village, owe you so much,' she said. 'I have heard from the hospital, they have arrived safely. Marc will have surgery on his hand later, the mother and child are doing well. Now Marthe here will bring a meal to your room. I suspect you will want a bath and to sleep. You have done very well and there is no need to worry about anything further. I will see that you are not disturbed.'

Thank goodness for efficiency, Lucy thought. She managed the meal, fell into the bath and then into bed. She slept at once.

Lucy woke at lunchtime and thought back over the past few hours. She felt almost detached from what had happened, distanced from all of the participants. It might have happened to someone else. And she knew what she had to do next.

She dressed and went downstairs. There was Simone, and Clotilde sitting with Lucille on her lap, showing more animation than she had done ever before.

'Lucy, are you all right?' Simone asked, 'I slept through it all, but when I woke up and there was this note from Marc, I was worried.'

'All right, Simone, don't excite yourself,' Clotilde said. 'I'm sure Lucy is better now she's rested. Now, Lucy, do sit down and we'll have tea in a moment. And before you ask, the hospital has been in touch again. Marc has had the operation on his hand. It was badly damaged, but they think that they have restored all movement, all feeling.'

'That's so good,' said Lucy. 'I was so worried.'

'We were all worried,' said Clotilde, showing no

sign of it. 'And the road has now been cleared so I'm going to see him in hospital in an hour.'

Tea was brought to them on a large silver tray. Lucy accepted a cup and said, 'Could you give me a lift? Then I will take the train to Lyon. I believe there is a good service.'

'Please! I thought you might like to stay a while. At least until you have recovered from your ordeal. And I know Marc will want to see you.'

'I've recovered now,' said Lucy, who hadn't. 'I really should get back. And I'm not needed any more for Simone or Lucille. Or Marc.'

'We still don't want you to go,' said Simone, but Lucy knew that her wishes now didn't count for too much.

'Would you like to call in to see Marc in the hospital?' Clotilde asked.

'There's no need. He needs his family now. I'll see him when he gets back to England.'

'As you wish. We will leave in an hour.'

'It won't take me long to pack,' said Lucy.

She knew she was still in a half-dream state. She had seen it before when people had had a shock. It took a couple of days before they realised the full enormity of what had happened.

There was a final goodbye to Simone and Lucille. Clotilde told her that she would see to the borrowed clothes and those Lucy had abandoned in the farmhouse would be sent on to her, along with her abandoned midwife's bag. Then it was into another large car, driven by a chauffeur. Clotilde was dropped off at the hospital.

'I say again,' Clotilde said, 'that I would like you

to stay. I know Marc would too.' But in spite of all her protests, Lucy insisted on being driven to the airport at Lyon.

Madame phoned ahead and reserved a seat on a flight to England.

Some time later Lucy landed in Manchester. She was travelling light, it was easy to take a train from the airport. Another hour and she was a bus ride from home.

She could have gone to stay with her parents. But she wanted—she needed—to be alone. She got to her room at nine that night. She had a shower, made cocoa, sat on the bed. Then she burst into tears.

Next morning she went to Jenny's office. 'I'm back and I'm fine and I need to start work at once,' she said.

Jenny looked up. 'I've heard from this French hospital,' she said. 'What's this about you practising abroad? Don't they have midwives of their own?'

'None in the area when we needed one,' said Lucy. 'Have you…? Did you hear about Marc's hand?'

Jenny frowned. 'Apparently the hand was a mess. He'll be there a while. But he'd not be much use to us here without two hands. Still, they say they'll let us know.'

She leaned back in her chair, looked up at Lucy. 'You can tell me all about it later—but for now, how did you get on with Marc?'

'I got on fine. I was just doing a job. Now, am I back in the delivery suite?'

* * *

It was good to be back in harness, working hard took her mind off things. She was doing a good job, helping with the births of fine, squalling babies, in safe, comfortable, hygienic conditions. This was the work she had chosen. But occasionally she thought back. She remembered how she had been in a rocking house, halfway up a mountain, not knowing whether she was going to live or die. And she had never felt more alive. Because she had been with Marc.

It was three days since she had returned, she had finished the day's shift and now she lay on her bed and thought. Once again she had turned down an invitation to go to the Red Lion and have a quiet—or loud—drink with a few friends. This avoidance of a social life was not like her. But for the moment she had just lost interest in that kind of thing.

She thought about Marc, and how she had told him she still loved him, when she had thought they had been in danger. It was true, of course. But she now realised that saying it had brought it out into the open. She couldn't deny it to herself now.

He had told her that their affair could go no further because of his commitment to the village. Now she had met his mother, seen the village and met some of the villagers, she understood what he meant. He—or someone—was needed there.

In fact, on the last day, when the sun had come out and she had seen the valley in all its beauty, she had felt an attraction. But he was right. She would not be happy there, she was a people person.

But she loved Marc. There was no getting away from it, she loved Marc. And seeing him at his best had made her love him more. He knew what he had to do and he was going to do it.

She closed her eyes, leaned back. She could see him in her mind's eye. She could remember every last detail—his eyes, his hair, his body... Leaning back in his chair as they had eaten under an umbrella in southern France. Or looking at her in the back of the car, when he had thought her asleep. Or when she had stayed the night at his flat and they had... She was torturing herself. This was foolish!

There was a knock on the door. June, down the corridor, had said she wanted to borrow a book so it would be her. 'Come in, June,' she called.

Lucy heard the door open and a voice said, 'It's not June. Will I do?'

She jerked upright, stared in shock at the man in the doorway. It was Marc! Just as she had been dreaming. Perhaps his face was a little thinner and his arm was in a sling. But it was certainly Marc. 'What are you doing here?' she asked stupidly.

'I came to see you. As soon as I could.'

She still had difficulty believing he was really there. 'But I thought you had to stay in hospital?'

'I'm a doctor. I can talk other doctors round. I've been transferred to the neurological department here.'

He came to sit next to her, put his uninjured arm round her shoulders and pulled her to him. 'Besides, I told them that the very best therapy possible for me was here. Remember how Simone seemed to improve when she got to the castle? Well, it's the same here with me. Though for different reasons.'

Then he kissed her. For a moment, for as long as he wanted to. She was willing to let him. But then she had to ease him away. 'Marc, we can't do this! And it was you that decided, not me.'

Mildly he said, 'You changed the rules halfway up a wet mountain. You kissed me, told me you loved me!'

'That was different! I was afraid that we might die at any minute.'

'Aren't people supposed to tell the truth when they're about to die? Were you telling the truth? Do you still love me?''

'Yes, but... Marc, please, don't do this to me,' she sobbed. 'Haven't I suffered enough?'

His face was contrite. 'Lucy, sweetheart, I'm so sorry. The last thing I want is for you to suffer. I've suffered myself, I know what it's like.'

She couldn't stop him when he quickly kissed her again Then he said, quite clearly, 'Lucy Stephens, I love you.'

'What?' Was she hearing things?

'Well, if you can say it, so can I,' he pointed out reasonably. 'I'll say it again. Lucy Stephens, I love you.'

'But I thought you said... And after seeing you in Montreval... And knowing what it's like, and your mother and I...'

'I have my own life to lead,' he said. 'And I want to lead it with you. For the moment we're both a bit damaged, perhaps we both need time. But when you said you loved me, and then had to go and see to Helene, I thought I knew what was most important in my life. You were. I felt a great rush when you said it, as if everything had been made clear to me. You had to be the most important thing in my life. You are more important to me than Montreval. Lucy, nothing can keep us apart. We can work it all out.'

'I thought I'd been happy before,' Lucy said, 'but it was never like this.' And she knew she was truly happy. The tears were pouring down her cheeks.

She leaned over to kiss him. 'I told you I loved you,' she pointed out, 'and what did you do then? You went to sleep.'

'So much for the great French lover. Look, you've got a lot of forgiving to do. But if you can forgive me...and if I can persuade you to...'

Another knock on the door. Marc looked at her. She took a book from her desk, walked over to the door and partially opened it, then thrust the book through the narrow gap. 'Here, June,' she said. 'It's a good read. I'm really tired now, going straight to bed.' A big artificial yawn. 'See you in the morning.'

'We won't be disturbed now,' she told Marc.

'You said you were going to bed.'

'So I did. And you were talking about forgiving. Well, I have. Now I'm going to bed and you're forgiven.'

'I'm glad about that.'

'Remember, after I kissed you in the farmhouse, you went to sleep? Well, you've just kissed me. So I want to go to sleep. I want to go to bed anyway. Are you tired, too?'

'Not too tired,' he said. Then he reached inside the neck of her shirt, gently eased out the gold chain. There was the medallion. 'Love conquers all,' he said.

EPILOGUE

IT HAD been a frantic, hard-working, supremely happy three months. Now Christmas would soon be on them. 'Good time for making an announcement,' he said. 'Shall we go and look at rings again?'

They had spent two or three very enjoyable mornings wandering through jewellers' shops. They'd compared the relative merits of antique rings, modern rings, gold, platinum, solitaire, cluster—and so far had come to no decision.

'Well, it always makes me feel pleased with life. But are we in a hurry?'

'Your mother is. She keeps on telling me that if anyone should want to hire a big hall for any reason—not that she can think of any reason—they ought to remember it gets booked up quite quickly.'

'My mother is always the diplomat. She likes to put things nicely but get her meaning across. She'd like an engagement party.'

'So would I,' he said. 'And my mother feels the same. She thinks a lot of you. She wants to see you again, soon. And she wants an heir for the estate.'

'Making your mother a grandmother is not the most pressing of arguments,' Lucy said, 'but I suspect she'd be good as one.'

There was not much chance of either of them having much time off over Christmas. It was generally accepted that staff with children should be given priority, especially on Christmas Day. But they were both invited to the big Christmas supper at Lucy's parents'.

'We can take some time off in January if you like,' she said. 'You can take me to visit your mother. Get her used to the idea of us as a couple.'

'She likes the idea. She's been planning, working out our future.'

Lucy blinked. 'She has?'

'We're a five-hundred-year-old family. She likes you a lot. But more than that, she thinks you'll be a fine mother, producing fine heirs for the Montreval dynasty. She thinks you have the qualities we need.'

'Makes me feel like a brood mare,' said Lucy. But she was secretly pleased.

They had talked for hours about his feeling that he ought to go back to Montreval. Lucy had said that she was willing to go, they should share everything, the bad things as much as the good. He said he only wanted her to be happy, and he didn't think that she'd be happy in a French village with hardly any young people. And so far they had come to no conclusion.

'We will cope,' she said gently. 'Just remember, all that really matters is that we have each other.'

He kissed her. 'That is all that matters.'

That conversation had been on a Monday night. On Wednesday she was working lates. Marc said he'd pick her up at the end of the shift. Perhaps for a while they could go to one of the many pre-Christmas parties at the Red Lion.

But when he arrived she could tell that he was excited about something. He kissed her, not caring who saw them. He wrapped his arms round her, hugged her and said, 'Never mind the Red Lion. Tonight is just for us. I've got something exciting to show you.'

'A ring?' she asked, half-hopefully. But she had wanted to help choose it herself.

'Not a ring. Something better than a ring. We're going back to my flat.'

He wouldn't tell her more. He drove them back to his flat where there was a bottle of very good champagne waiting in a bucket of ice. He popped the cork, filled two glasses. 'Here's to us and our happy future. A future that is now a lot more certain.'

'Marc, you're doing this on purpose! I want to know what's happened! I can see that you're happy—make me happy, too. Why is our future now a lot more certain?'

He fetched a large envelope, took a map from it and spread it on the table.

'Look, here's the map showing Montreval. A dead end. A tiny village, cut off for much of the winter, little work, little amusement. No one much goes there.'

He took a red pen, scored a line along the valley bottom to Montreval and then inked in a series of red dots after that.

'I've just heard from my uncle, Jules Romilly—you know, the lawyer, Simone's father. The one who keeps an eye on our affairs. He says that the government has given money to build a spur off the motorway, take it along the valley and through Montreval, dig a tunnel at the far end and connect us to the main skiing area. Work will start in spring. Montreval will be the centre of operations. There'll be many people flooding in, lots of work. Prosperity for everyone.'

'Are you pleased? Won't this mean that the Comte de Montreval will no longer be needed?'

'I'm delighted. My mother can retire, take an interest but no longer run the place. My uncle has approached her, they're thinking of turning the castle into a hotel. And I...'

'You're not needed,' she said.

'I can choose! If I practise medicine there, I can build and open the clinic I've always wanted. Or I can have a career in obs and gynae. I love it! Or even both! Now, how can we celebrate?'

'Let's choose a ring,' she said.

MILLS & BOON®

1205/03b

Live the emotion

Medical romance™

THE NURSE'S SECRET SON by *Amy Andrews*

Nurse Sophie Monday is the mother of a small boy – a boy everyone believes to be her late husband Michael's. But once she loved his brother Daniel, and when tragedy struck he rejected her, unaware she was carrying his baby. Now Daniel's back – and Sophie must admit the truth!

A&E DRAMA: *Pulses are racing in these fast-paced dramatic stories*

THE SURGEON'S RESCUE MISSION by *Dianne Drake*

Solaina saved Dr David Gentry's life when she found him injured in the jungle. As she nursed him back to health he nurtured feelings in her she'd never known. But soon they find themselves in a dangerous situation that could cost them their lives – and the lives of their patients!

24:7 *Feel the heat – every hour...every minute... every heartbeat*

THE PREGNANT GP by *Judy Campbell*

Lisa Balfour has come to Arrandale to be the town's GP. She soon finds herself attracted to gorgeous doctor Ronan Gillespie – but one night of passion results in her pregnancy, and she's faced with a heart-wrenching dilemma. She must keep her pregnancy a secret...

On sale 6th January 2006

Available at most branches of WHSmith, Tesco, ASDA, Borders, Eason, Sainsbury's and most bookshops

Visit www.millsandboon.co.uk

FREE!

4 Books
and a surprise gift!

We would like to take this opportunity to thank you for reading this Mills & Boon® book by offering you the chance to take FOUR more specially selected titles from the Medical Romance™ series absolutely FREE! We're also making this offer to introduce you to the benefits of the Reader Service™—

- ★ **FREE home delivery**
- ★ **FREE gifts and competitions**
- ★ **FREE monthly Newsletter**
- ★ **Exclusive Reader Service offers**
- ★ **Books available before they're in the shops**

Accepting these FREE books and gift places you under no obligation to buy. you may cancel at any time, even after receiving your free shipment. Simply complete your details below and return the entire page to the address below. You don't even need a stamp!

YES! Please send me 4 free Medical Romance books and a surprise gift. I understand that unless you hear from me, I will receive 6 superb new titles every month for just £2.75 each, postage and packing free. I am under no obligation to purchase any books and may cancel my subscription at any time. The free books and gift will be mine to keep in any case.

M5ZEF

Ms/Mrs/Miss/Mr .... Initials ....

BLOCK CAPITALS PLEASE

Surname ....

Address ....

....

.... Postcode ....

Send this whole page to:
UK: FREEPOST CN81, Croydon, CR9 3WZ